A Very Wrong Number

In the computer room of a provincial university Peter Helinger dials a wrong number and is connected to the computer of a major bank. At the touch of a key he could transfer sums in and out of accounts leaving no trace of how it was done.

The university is so short of funds that there is a very real threat that jobs will go. With two like-minded colleagues Helinger decides to remedy this by transferring a large sum from a seemingly inactive account into the university's coffers and passing it off as an anonymous bequest.

But the account was inactive because its holder had opened it with the proceeds of a spectacular fraud for which he had served time. His sentence now over, he plans to reactivate his bank account. But he knows that both the police and the criminal fraternity want to get their hands on the unrecovered money.

When he discovers that the account is virtually empty, the number of possible culprits is myriad, and because of his behaviour the bank itself discovers that their security is far from foolproof.

Before long Helinger and his friends are in deep trouble and being hunted by several people. Their amateur act of thievery leads them into a world of professional violence. Luckily for them Jonathan Craythorne puts his military professionalism on their side, but not before the trio fall into the hands of some very determined and ruthless men.

Once again Arthur Douglas (author of *The Goods* and *Last Rights*) has produced a fast and humorous adventure whose solution is wholly satisfactory.

by the same author

**THE GOODS
LAST RIGHTS**

Arthur Douglas

A VERY WRONG NUMBER

MACMILLAN
LONDON

First published 1987 by
MACMILLAN LONDON LIMITED
4 Little Essex Street London WC2R 3LF
and Basingstoke

Associated companies in Auckland, Delhi, Dublin, Gaborone,
Hamburg, Harare, Hong Kong, Johannesburg, Kuala Lumpur, Lagos,
Manzini, Melbourne, Mexico City, Nairobi, New York, Singapore
and Tokyo

British Library Cataloguing in Publication Data

Douglas, Arthur, *1926–*
    A very wrong number.
    Rn: Gerald Hammond   I. Title
    823'.914[F]   PR6058.A55456

ISBN 0-333-42795-5

Typeset by
Bookworm Typesetting, Manchester

Printed and bound by
Anchor Brendon Ltd., Essex.

ONE

Leo Gunn had no great objection to being in prison. If he had resented his incarceration he was big enough and hard enough to have left nobody in any doubt about it, but in fact he regarded it as no more than a fair exchange. He had obtained a large sum of money and he had done so by means of which the law disapproved. The law had therefore required that, for his part of the bargain, he spend some time in a place not of his own choice.

Fair enough. Anything is tolerable, he thought, if one has something to look forward to. And he had. By God he had! Meantime, he would catch up on his reading and thinking. Even the absence of women was no worse than a slightly mixed blessing.

A lesser man than Leo might have had cause to dread the day of his release. The fact that none of the money had been recovered was well known to the criminal fraternity, but so also was his unofficial record of killings and assaults. And, although he disapproved of hard work undertaken for no reward, he had made full use of the prison's gymnastic facilities to keep himself in trim despite the handicaps of prison diet and excess leisure. He was as fit, and his strength as great, as ever.

5

He could only think of one group which might try to carry him off to some lonely spot for interrogation and disposal and he would not have given much for their chances.

The law had never given up and never would. The perpetrators of far larger frauds might still be free, but they had remained within the law or had acted on a scale at which prosecution was unthinkable. Leo's fraud had been too large to be forgiven and too small to buy invulnerability. The loss had come to rest with an insurance company which had had not the least objection to prosecuting him and which, with typical wish to have its cake and eat it, also wanted its money back.

But that also was part of the game. Leo had had more than a dozen different cell-mates foisted on him, of whom at least half had been planted with the promise of an easier deal if they could get him to open his mouth. Tony Hayes, who had joined him only that morning, might be the eighth or maybe the ninth but he was certainly one of them. Otherwise, why was he being so affable? Years before, when Hayes had been an impecunious con-man and Leo a part-time enforcer, Hayes had been slow to repay the money which he had borrowed from Leo's boss of the moment to finance a caper. Leo, as instructed, had administered a beating of the first magnitude. And Hayes was not the man to forgive and forget.

Leo relaxed on the lower bunk – his weight, of solid bone and muscle with not an ounce of flab, was such as to make the use of an upper bunk unsafe – and decided to have a little fun with Hayes and with the microphone which was pretending to be a bolt beside the window-bars. Leo was not normally given to pranks, but prison life would have been unendurable without a little light relief.

'Tell 'em they're wasting their time,' he said suddenly.

He felt the jerk as the man in the upper bunk jumped. 'Aiee . . .' Hayes paused and pulled himself together. 'I beg your pardon?' Always polite was Tony Hayes.

'They're wasting their time. You got cloth ears?'

'Who are?'

Leo raised one foot and kicked the underside of the bunk above, almost lifting Hayes off the hard mattress. 'Don't give me none of that,' Leo said. 'You've got soft, these last years. But I'm as hard as ever I was. Hard as the last time I gave you a going-over. Don't want another, do you?'

Hayes' long face, white with apprehension, appeared over the side of the upper bunk. 'For Christ's sake, Leo, I don't know what you're on about. Honest.'

'Pull the other one,' Leo said. 'I know how these things go. I been part of them. Somebody wants to know where I put the money. Who you working for?' He nearly suggested a name but he caught himself in time. Mention of the Filbustini brothers might put ideas into certain heads.

'Nobody,' Hayes said.

'On your own account, are you?'

Hayes' face appeared again. 'I'm not working at all, believe me, Leo,' he said plaintively. 'I don't care where the money is. I'm just not interested. I don't want to know.'

'Just as well,' Leo grunted. 'It's out of the country. Always was. And they needn't bother to try and pick me up when I get out of here, because I'm being met. I'll be on a plane within an hour, passport and all. It's already paid for.'

He heard a faint creak as Hayes relaxed.

'Good for you, Leo,' Hayes said. 'I always said you

7

had more guile than they gave you credit for. But, if it's already paid for, how sure are you that they'll be there to meet you?'

'You know something I don't know?' Leo snapped. It took an effort to keep the amusement out of his voice.

The bunk twitched again. 'I don't know a damn thing,' Hayes said quickly. 'Just going from experience. If somebody's already been paid in advance, the berks don't usually bother to do the job.'

'Leaving me to be grabbed by whoever's pulling your strings? Forget it. I've got too much on them. The evidence is in a safe-deposit box,' Leo improvised, embellishing an already adequate invention, 'and the key's buried under a rose-bush in the gardens of Buckingham Palace.' Leo had nothing against Her Majesty, indeed he was rather in favour of the monarchy, but the Queen's name had figured large in the indictments against him, so it was only fair that she should bear a share of the aggro and inconvenience. 'All the same, I could do with knowing who sicked you on to me. You want to get out of here?'

'Course I do, Leo,' Hayes said huskily.

'And so you shall. You've got until this time tomorrow to tell me who it is. After that, I'll slide you under the door. Or maybe you meant alive?'

Leo relaxed, well content. Hayes, after a sleepless night, was removed to another cell-block in the morning.

TWO

Peter Helinger disposed, with some difficulty, of a visitor whom he regarded as no more than a passing irritant.

The man, from some trifling department in Applied Science, had brought him an elementary problem requiring only repeated integration for its solution. Peter had, in fact, solved it in his head while reading it, but he had too much innate courtesy to say so. He had solemnly put it into the computer and presented the foreseen answer to the supplicant with as much reverence as if it had been unleavened bread. Thereafter, he had to endure several minutes of misplaced gratitude and a lengthy discourse on university politics before his visitor took the last of several hints and departed.

Alone at last in the Computer Room, and with no engagements pending until a seminar late that afternoon, he decided to get on with the main task of the day.

A conventional telephone dial was set, incongruously, into the face of his console. Absently, while most of his considerable brain dissected the problem ahead, he dialled a number from memory. The VDU screen flickered and then showed, as it should, a logo followed by text; but neither the pattern nor the text was what he had expected.

He scratched his thatch of overlong, curly, brown hair while he brought his mind back from its mathematical lair.

'How very odd!' he said aloud. He put out his hand to break the connection and then paused and looked again. He rotated his swivel chair, picked up a telephone from the shelf behind him and dialled another number.

In the Department of Economics Building, Hector Westerly was concluding a lecture to a totally uninterested group of law students who had chosen Economics as an easy option to make up the requisite number of subjects.

Like Peter Helinger, he found it quite unnecessary to direct the whole of his intelligence into the more mundane aspects of his work. He was mentally replanning his garden while he spoke.

'And so,' he said, 'money, as currency, is no more than ... what?'

A voice from the back broke a deathly silence. 'Counters for goods and services,' it said.

'Or?'

The silence lasted a little longer this time. 'Or any record entitling the holder to the same purchasing-power,' the same voice said at last.

'Not quite as elegantly phrased as my own words, but near enough. It is only when money is treated as capital that it takes on a life of its own. Time enough next week to worry your legal brains with such mundane matters.'

The department secretary glimpsed his stocky figure and balding head and caught him at the bend of the stairs. 'Dr Westerly! Dr Helinger phoned.' She was a meticulous woman who had worked in other departments and was devoted to her job. She had total recall for degrees and honours, and never made a mistake by confusing professors, doctors (including the humblest and newest PhD but always excepting, of course, the occasional surgeon) or mere misters. 'You're invited to take coffee with him in the Computer Room.'

Hector Westerly stroked his neat beard and tried not to frown. He had intended a peaceful interlude in the Staff Club. 'I suppose I'd better go,' he said. 'But the computer makes such rotten coffee.'

The secretary laughed dutifully. It was part of the job, but she also had a slight fondness for the dapper lecturer.

Westerly crossed a quadrangle, took a short-cut through the modern Admin Building, paused to admire the spring flowers in a second quadrangle and then reluctantly, because it was a fine day after a spell of rain and wind, entered the more substantial building which housed, among others, the Department of Mathematics and Computing.

Computing had originally been an autonomous department, but its status had been eroded when the advent of the microchip had made the possession of an individual microcomputer not only possible but apparently essential for every department with pretensions to mathematical need. Computing had been absorbed into Mathematics, a liaison which one diehard statistician had likened to a marriage between the Hydrostatics Lab and Gregorian chant.

The customary emptiness of the Computer Room was not wholly due to this change of status. The six consoles were rarely in full use, but the apparatus whirred irregularly as other departments, whose needs exceeded the capacity of the microcomputer and whose budgets did not allow for access by telephone to larger mainframes and programs elsewhere, ran work through

11

the computer from satellite terminals in their own buildings.

A technician, wheeling a small trolley laden with tapes and discs, was leaving as Westerly arrived. He found Peter Helinger alone in the big room, brooding over the only live VDU while sipping at a mug of black coffee. The mug was enlivened by a picture of Snoopy.

Without waiting for an invitation, Westerly helped himself from the percolator on another trolley beside the door. He used his customary mug (Tom and Jerry), added sugar and cream and pulled up another chair beside the younger man. The two had first met over an intriguing problem in currency fluctuations and, finding common interests, had become firm if casual friends.

'What have you got for me?' Westerly asked.

'Ah,' Helinger said, returning to earth. 'There you are. I've come up on this, accidentally. Thought you might recognise the logo. Or the language. It looks like Combank. You know it, don't you?'

'I have a passing acquaintance. Let's have a look.' Westerly stared at the screen and took an absent-minded pull at his coffee. 'You really must get your technicians to clean out the apparatus some time.'

Peter Helinger looked surprised. 'It's all functioning perfectly,' he said.

'I meant the coffee apparatus.'

'I make the coffee around here.'

'Be ashamed. Yes,' Westerly said. 'I've seen this before. You've come up on the main computer of the National Bank. How in hell did you manage it? That number's supposed to be the most closely guarded secret after the date of the Second Coming. Their own staff only get to use an Autodial gadget.'

Helinger used one of his habitually vague gestures to indicate a stack of papers topped by a box of tape.

'Rumark, the chap who's doing that thing about airflow for Farnborough, tried to write his own program again. He asked me to de-bug it, which really means a re-write. Half of it overlaps part of the Interfit program which Imperial use. I was going to print out their program and see what bits I could use.'

'Steal, you mean,' Westerly said without censure. Such expedients were common practice.

'Sticks and stones. I dialled from memory.'

'London. Same district. What's Imperial's number?'

This time, Helinger consulted a list. 'Three two seven five.'

Westerly rolled his chair along to an adjacent console, switched on and keyed in. 'With a four-figure number,' he said, 'the most likely error would be to reverse second and third digits. I'll try it.' He dialled. The screen continued obstinately to imitate a distant snow-fall but the ringing tone was followed by a mellifluous female voice from a small speaker.

Westerly plugged in the microphone which nestled in a recess in the console. After a brief, flirtatious chat, he disconnected.

'Randy sod!' Helinger said.

'Thank you. But for my own approaching nuptials, I would have pursued the matter further. Ah well, I can find the number again, should any hitch develop. We'll try reversing the third and fourth.' He dialled again. This time, a display appeared which matched that on the other screen. 'Got it! This could make an interesting teaching tool.' He switched off the second console and trundled himself back. 'Of course, we aren't even on program yet. See if I can remember my Combank . . .' He poised over the keyboard like a heron at a stream and then keyed in five digits. 'There you are, my boy. A menu.'

Dr Helinger examined the menu – a numbered list of facilities – with professional interest. 'And I could guess who wrote it,' he said.

'I know who wrote it.'

'Don't tell me. You remember that conference on Computer Security we went to at Hammersmith?'

'Vaguely. We hit the night-spots.'

'Didn't we, just! One of the speakers was from National Bank. Boforth, that was the name. He came over as a bit of a dimwit in some ways, but clever at his own line.'

'That could be said of many of our colleagues,' Westerly said. 'Present company, of course, excepted.'

'That goes without saying. Anyway, he showed us some of his own programming. He used "Tape" instead of "Spool", and "Store" instead of "Save". Am I right?'

'Spot on,' Westerly said.

'Shall we try to go deeper? Let's try Commodity Transactions.'

'No harm trying.'

Helinger keyed. The screen went blank. 'Damn it,' he said mildly. 'There's a security code. So the menu's as far as we can get.'

'Let's not give up yet,' Westerly said. 'Isn't young Polly Holt doing something on security codes? She might be able to break through. Would she be in the Staff Club?'

Helinger looked at his watch and then turned to pick up the phone. 'She usually spends her between-lectures times in her room, designing uncopyable programs for the video-games people. I'll try.'

Pauline Holt joined them within a few minutes, a small female in her middle twenties. Nature had not intended her to be unattractive, but her own efforts had confounded those of nature. She wore her hair twisted into an inelegant knot and was given to lopsided tweed skirts worn with discordant peasant blouses and no makeup. Her heavy spectacles were ill-chosen. This neglect of appearance was generally taken to be a signal that she would prefer not to be made the subject of gallantry, and the wish was respected.

She declined coffee and trundled up another chair.

'We have an interesting little academic problem,' Westerly said. 'We can get on to the National Bank mainframe computer, and we can get as far as the menu.' He demonstrated. 'Beyond that point, we're up against security codes. Do I recall that you came under Vernon Boforth while he was still working out of Cambridge?'

'Not directly,' Polly said. She had a pleasant, slightly husky voice. 'But my tutor, Donald Lambsden, was under him. And Dr Lambsden wasn't always discreet. He used some of their programming among his lecture notes.'

'Can you break through, then?'

'I think so.' She removed her spectacles and stared unseeingly in the distance. 'Not by trial-and-error. That would take ages. It would be easier to dump out the program on to paper and take a look at it.'

'That would take years,' Dr Helinger protested.

'It might. But I might get a breakthrough within a few hours,' she said. 'Remember, I'd know which bits I was looking for. But it would still be a hell of a lot of work. I'd want your assurance that it was worthwhile as an academic exercise. Or – forgive me, doctors – this is only academic?' She replaced her glasses and looked from one to the other with the anxious expression of an emerging mole.

'Yes, of course it is,' Helinger said.

'Not necessarily,' said Westerly at almost the same

moment. He hesitated before going on. 'Think for a moment. What do you consider to be the country's most desperate need at the moment?' The habit of teaching by questions was hard to break.

'Education,' said Miss Holt, and Helinger gave a grunt of agreement.

'Quite so,' said Westerly. 'Increasing leisure. Rising aspirations. Competition in world markets. We should be teaching our youth to pull their weight in this technological world, to make full use of their new leisure and to contribute to the standard of life world-wide, not turning them out, half-baked, to idleness and glue-sniffing. So what is our opinion of the present Government cuts?'

'Damnable,' said Helinger. Polly gave a quick nod.

'And,' Westerly said, 'as I recall a document on which University Court deferred decision at its last meeting, your job, Polly, is on the line. And yours, Helinger, none too safe.' It was by tradition that males were addressed by their surnames, females by first names.

Polly Holt broke a heavy silence. 'It may be all for the best,' she said. 'Get out of a rut. Might go to the States.'

'Do you really want to uproot yourself from your comfortable little niche and flush yourself down the brain drain?'

'The choice is hardly in my hands,' she pointed out. 'But it's the last thing in the world I'd want. Of course it is. My life is here.'

'You could command a much higher salary.'

'What on earth would I spend it on?'

The question, rhetorical as it was, disorientated Westerly for a moment. He had never expected to hear a girl utter such heresy. But then, Polly Holt was a very odd person. 'You could take a hand in the matter. Think about it. The Vice Chancellor has just emerged from his

16

ivory tower and is desperately trying to raise a hundred thousand quid to bridge over the coming year, rather than achieve the required savings by losing staff who could never be replaced. It's not a big sum, although he's making heavy weather of it.'

'It seems big enough from where I stand,' Polly said.

'Peanuts!' Westerly nodded at the console. 'One per cent on all the service charges would never be missed. And it would cover the deficit handsomely. And where would the loss end up? Back with the Government, who started the rot.'

'It's not possible,' Polly said. 'We'd be found out.'

Peter Helinger had been listening in silence, but now he roused himself. 'I'm not saying that I agree with Dr Westerly, but I don't go along with you either. Westerly and I were at a conference on Computer Security last year,' he said. 'I had lunch with a man from the London branch of one of the big American banks. He reckoned that his bank was losing between ten and twenty million dollars a year to computer frauds. He couldn't even put it closer than that. They're trying to develop means to stop it, so far without any success.'

'Look at it another way,' said Westerly. He was infecting himself with his own enthusiasm. 'Suppose that one of us were to use this keyboard to take, say, one pound from each of a hundred thousand accounts and credit the sum to the University's account. And we tell the computer to leave the amount but to forget the transaction. You follow me? The University is only told of an anonymous benefaction. It's just conceivable that somebody could question the origin of that entry. It's virtually impossible that he could prove anything amiss. And it's inconceivable that anybody could ever prove which individual sat down at which keyboard and gave the computer its instructions.'

17

'I see.' Miss Holt removed her glasses again, and with them ten years from her apparent age. 'This needs thinking about,' she said. 'I need time.'

'Of course you do,' Westerly said. 'We all do. But, meantime, you might just do a little exploration to see whether you're as good as you think you are. We wouldn't be committed to anything. But I'd hate to waste my precious mental resources in ethical argument only to find that you couldn't "hack in" – that is the right word? – past Boforth's safeguards.'

Polly's chin went up. 'If that's what you think,' she said, 'you're in for a shock.'

Despite her Parthian shot, Polly Holt procrastinated. In theory, the suggested research would not commit her; in practice, she doubted her own ability to withstand persuasion from her two seniors.

A phone-call from her father put the matter out of her mind. Her ailing mother had taken a turn for the worse. She filled up her Mini and went home for a long weekend.

The old house was no longer the home which it had once been. During the weeks since Mrs Holt had last been able to descend the stairs, the daily help had been efficient; but cleanliness and order were no substitute for loving care.

Mrs Holt lay where she had chosen, in a large upstairs bedroom which overlooked the long garden which she had planted and nurtured since Polly was a baby. The garden was getting out of hand now, for Mr Holt did not have the interest, the time or the magic touch, but she could still admire from her window the fruit trees, coming now into blossom, and the bright splashes of the early flowers.

Polly sat with her mother, read to her and chatted by the hour, which at least gave her father a respite. Since

Polly's interests were mathematical and her friends were all university staff whom her parents had never met, the chatter was incomprehensible to Mrs Holt. Nevertheless, she nodded and even smiled, relieved to see her awkward daughter settled at last. All that was needed now was a husband, but if the girl would go around looking like an eccentric aunt made young again . . .

When the invalid was settled for the night, father and daughter sat down for a quiet gin. 'I'm glad you could come,' Mr Holt said. 'I'd hardly been out of the house for a fortnight, and your visits always do her so much good.'

'I only hope I can keep coming,' Polly said. There was no point in trying to break it gently. Her father had always been able to take it on the chin. 'We're facing staff cuts. If it comes to the worst . . .'

'There are other jobs,' her father said.

'Not in my line, and not here. It would mean abroad. The States. Silicon Valley.'

From the corner of her eye, she watched her father strive to put a brave face on it and she suddenly knew that this time the effort was almost too much. She felt tears behind her eyes. The rock on which her family had flourished had been eroded by the years. 'If you must go, you must,' he said at last. 'Your mother won't want to keep you back.'

'I'll be making more,' she said. Dr Westerly's remark took on fresh significance. 'I could afford to fly back quite often.'

'I hope so.'

'Or you could both come with me?' She would have said anything to try to soften this blow.

'Your mother would never leave here. And how could we afford the cost of medical care over there? No, my dear, we'll let her live out her days here, where she

19

has been happy. Just . . . just try to come back as often as you can.'

'Maybe it won't come to that,' she said.

The daffodils were gone, tulips were almost over and the first of the rosebuds were beginning to burst before Hector Westerly crossed the quiet quadrangle to the Computer Room to attend a progress meeting. Previous reports had been of a total lack of progress, but this time was understood to be different.

The day was Sunday. The Students' Union was half-alive but in the academic buildings only the occasional researcher with a long-running project made quiet encroachment on the Sabbath calm.

The Maths Building was otherwise deserted but in the Computer Room he found Peter Helinger, lost in a paperback, and Polly Holt. Polly seemed to have dressed, as usual, in cast-offs designed for a pre-war Church Social nature-ramble and her hair was uncombed.

She also seemed to be unwontedly nervous. 'Look, are you sure you want to go any further?' she demanded. 'What I've already done is illegal, immoral and unethical. The Nineteen Eighty Four Data Protection Act alone—'

Westerly took one of the vacant chairs. 'Tell us what you've done,' he said, 'and we'll judge for ourselves.'

'Well . . .' Polly took off her glasses, stared at him myopically and put them back on again. 'I suppose. I couldn't get anywhere at first. Everything seemed to be protected up to the hilt. And whenever you make a wrong move you get cut off and have to dial again. But I knew that there aren't too many codes for dumping out a program in its basic notation and you wouldn't expect it to be so well protected because there aren't that many people could make sense of it anyway.' She paused for breath. 'And after a lot of trial-and-error I suddenly got the printer to deliver about a hundred-weight of gibberish.'

'And that gave you the lot?'

'It turned out to be a program for monitoring the performance of the bank's industrial borrowers. But at least it gave me a clue as to how to get the rest of the programs dumped. That produced another ton of gibberish to be unscrambled the hard way.' She paused and waited for expressions of amazement.

'Golly!' Westerly said obligingly.

'Golly is right,' Polly said, removing her glasses again. Without them, she had the look of a plain but intelligent child. 'It was a hell of a sweat. But would you believe this? After all the protection they'd given the system, with a randomly selected security code for each day up to the end of the millenium, they'd stored those codes in the computer instead of feeding them in manually every day. Once I got that out, I knew that it was only a matter of time.'

'And now,' Westerly said, 'what can you do?'

'She can make it sing hymns,' said Helinger, looking up suddenly from his book.

'If I want to,' Polly said. 'And I'm not at all sure that I do. I've gone far enough outside the law already.' Her eyes were defiant and her face was very pink.

'See if you can get anywhere with her,' Helinger said. 'I keep coming up against a brick wall. I think she has a security code woven into her DNA.'

The pink flushed scarlet. 'And I'm disappointed in you,' she snapped. 'I thought you were above trying to persuade me into crime.'

'My job's on the line too.'

Westerly looked from one to the other with his sharp

little eyes. 'My dear,' he said, 'we respect your scruples. And nobody's trying to turn you into a female space-age Horatio Bottomley. But surely, after all the effort you've put in, you'll demonstrate that you really could break into it?'

The slight doubt in his voice stung her on the raw. Without comment, she slid her chair in front of the console, dialled and then keyed digits. The screen flickered and settled. 'There you are,' she said. 'The University's current-account balance.'

Peter Helinger looked in surprise. 'It's not a lot, is it?' he said.

'Of course it isn't,' Westerly said impatiently. 'Any large sums should be on deposit where they earn interest. Polly, show us what you can do. Could you find us a large current account where there have been no recent transactions.'

Back on her familiar territory, Polly Holt lowered her guard. She became interested. She opened a fat, loose-leaf book and leafed through it until she found what she wanted. She keyed again. 'I can let the computer find it for you.'

'Why no recent transactions?' Helinger asked.

'Because anyone who leaves a large sum on current account for a long period has to be a crook,' Westerly said. 'The only reason for forgoing interest would be to avoid having the bank make its statutory report to the Inland Revenue.'

'It could have belonged to a businessman who died in the middle of a big deal.'

'Possibly. But if his heirs didn't know about it, they won't miss it.'

'How about this one?' Polly said suddenly. 'No transactions since the bank went computerised, five and a half years ago.'

Westerly looked at the screen. 'Beautiful!' he said. 'A hundred and fifty-one thousand, three hundred and eighty-two plus a few odd pence. Who does it belong to?'

Polly keyed again. 'Hong Kong Property Development Trust. No address.'

'Could be genuine,' said Helinger. 'With the mainland Chinese getting a foothold soon, capital must be flooding out.'

'That's what somebody wanted his banker to think, five years ago,' Westerly said. 'But no Chinese would dream of leaving that much money idle for so long. They believe, devoutly, that money and women should work for them. And the lack of an address for the sending of statements is a giveaway. It could even be the ill-gotten gains of somebody who's died during his sentence. Polly, just suppose, for the sake of academic interest, that you were going to transfer some money into the University's account. Could you leave the new balance but erase all memory of the transaction?'

'Very easily,' she said. 'I won't do it, but let's suppose for the sake of some more academic interest that I did. How on earth would you square it with the University?'

'That's the easy bit,' Westerly said. 'I see from *The Times* that the solicitor who sold my last house for me has passed into whatever dusty heaven lawyers go to. He was a one-man band and his office has now closed. I would photocopy his letterhead on to a fresh sheet of paper and type a letter to the Vice Chancellor telling him that the money had been deposited to the University's account as an anonymous benefaction, with only two conditions. First, that the money be used to avert the threatened redundancies. And, second, that no enquiries whatever be made as to the identity of the benefactor, not by reference to the solicitor nor even an

23

acknowledgement. And I would spread a carefully composed rumour about some former graduate who's struck it big in oil or uranium and remembered his Alma Mater.'

'That's clever,' Polly admitted. 'But I still won't do it.' She set her lips in a firm line.

'Nobody's asking you to do anything,' Westerly said. 'But if you have any feeling for this throne of learning, if you want it to continue in the forefront where it's become established through the efforts of such as yourself, and if you want to save a great many school-leavers from being robbed of the chance of further education, and above all if you don't want to find yourself and some of your colleagues – including men with families – dumped in the dole-queue or forced to take their talents abroad, you'll go for a walk, leaving that book where it is.'

There was silence in the room, broken only by a faint hiss from the massed electronics. 'No,' Polly said at last. 'It's not honest. And I suspect my own motives.'

Westerly sighed. 'If that's how you feel, so be it. Although it's a pity that all your work should be wasted. But you're a good girl, Polly. Your parents should be proud of you.'

Without knowing it, he had used the proper pass-word. The silence stretched out for a full minute. Then Polly got to her feet and clumped out of the room, leaving her papers on the bench.

THREE

Despite his bulk, Leo Gunn came out of the tube and crossed the concourse of the main line station like a rabbit leaving its burrow. The first of the ferrets was not far behind him.

He dived for the taxi rank. At that hour, while commuters were still scurrying for home it was a safe bet that taxis would be available. If there were a queue, he would be thwarted again. At six foot four and nearly twenty stone, he was too damned easy to follow on foot, but the journey by tube had been necessary. The radios of the followers would not have worked from so far beneath London and he had bought a ticket to the end of the line.

By now the three unmarked police cars which had started on his tail would be homing in. And the chase had already made a hole in the thirty-odd quid which had been in his pocket when he left Brixton Prison that morning. He needed to replenish his funds from the secret hoard but he would have died rather than lead his pursuers to it. It had been the focus of his hopes for too long. For twelve years, in fact, less a minimum of time off for good behaviour. His Ludship had taken Leo's flat refusal to reveal the whereabouts of his haul as a personal affront.

Luck was with him this time. Of the three taxis on the rank, the first had a fare and was already pulling out. He pushed a fiver into the hand of the driver of the third. 'Follow me,' he said. 'I got another fare for you.' His voice had a superficial gloss as of a minor public school, but as always in times of stress his native Glasgow peeped through, and his syntax was unpolished.

He jumped into the taxi which had been the middle of the three and barked the first address which came into his head. He looked back as they pulled away. The other cab was following and no others were coming up the ramp. The first of the detectives on his heels was running a losing race between the pedestrians. Even as he watched, the man swerved to avoid a dog on a lead and took a toss which would have made the reputation of a stunt-man. It looked like an Outpatient job.

Leo faced the front. If his former cronies could have seen his face they would have been amazed. They had never seen a smile on his flat, almost Ukrainian face. He was not quite smiling now but his habitual scowl had softened. Now all that he needed was another Underground station.

Leo Gunn had first seen the murky light of Clydeside some forty years before. He was the youngest child of the family – his still handsome mother had already been a widow for considerably more then the longest known period of gestation.

As is true of us all, Leo's life had been shaped by a thousand twists of fate. The first had been that, although he had no brothers, he had no less than six older sisters. The family was Catholic and paid lip-service to the faith and yet the house reeked of animal femininity. Virtue and virginity were highly praised but abortions, although unmentioned, were not unknown.

Leo was a tough and resilient youth and, having

passed the size and strength of the average male by the age of twelve, was well able to look after himself. But, at home, any readiness to assert his independence by using his superior strength was met by a torrent of reproach and the imposition of dietary sanctions.

Such a degree of female domination was too much for Leo to stomach. He spent as much time as he could out of the house, safe from those shrill and unstoppable voices, running with the tougher local gangs. At the first chance, he ran away to sea as a deckhand, firstly on a coaster and later on vessels bound for foreign parts.

With such a background it would not have been surprising if Leo had turned homosexual, but although he had a deep-rooted fear of women they were still the objects of his lust. Men failed to attract him.

A seaman's life suited him well. It gave him adventure and a look at the world, the chance of a little profitable smuggling or a satisfying dockside brawl whenever he could find an opponent to face up to one of his strength and reputation. And he could sate his considerable virility on compliant whores to whom, at least overtly, the customer was always right.

But no life is perfect. There is always a snag. Leo's was that, although he learned to control it, he never overcame seasickness. Others might find their sea-legs within the first two days of the voyage; after a month at sea, it still took only the smallest motion to set Leo hanging overside.

The company with which he had served for most of his time was sympathetic. He was a rough diamond but, despite his disability, Leo had taken his Mate's Ticket. They offered him an office job.

The office, with its regular hours, lower pay and preponderance of female staff was hell to Leo, but he stuck it out. He was learning all the time about the world of the sea which, it appeared, did not stop at the shore-line. Here was where the money was, but not for him. Eventually he was caught helping himself to some of the firm's and they parted company.

But the fringes of the sea still called. Leo took to the docks. His knowledge of ships, and his brute strength, made him useful as a docker but more useful to the criminal element. He was drawn into the battleground of labour organisation, the stealing and re-setting of goods in transit and thence into other areas of crime, murder and extortion not excluded. His education and intelligence advanced him, but not so fast as did his quick temper and savage strength. Soon he was leading his own gang.

Paradoxically, his downfall was due to his hankering for the more respectable life. After a decade of violent crime unsullied by convictions or even by arrest, he returned to a career in the world of marine business.

His time in the shipping office had not been wasted. His first three charter-party frauds went undetected. The fourth was too large to slip by. Even so, he had the money in his hand for a fortnight before suspicion arose and he was arrested, by which time the money had vanished. So also had Maurice Higgs, a close friend and henchman of the notorious Filbustini brothers. Maurie had last been seen when the brothers set him on Leo's trail in the hope of getting their hands on a share, if not the whole, of Leo's haul.

Those of the law were not the only ferrets in pursuit of the rabbit. The word had been spread among street-cleaners and dustmen, newsvendors and the carriers of sandwich-boards, ticket touts, street-traders and all the riff-raff of London that news of Leo's whereabouts was wanted and that rewards were available in cash or kind. Few of them would have known

Leo's face, but he was easy to describe and the clothes in which he had left prison were known.

Thus, shortly after the official pursuers were shaken off, others picked up the trail.

Sensing that he was still being followed but unaware that identities had changed, shaken by the unexpected talent and persistence of the police and with his earlier familiarity with the Underground system now clouded by time, Leo made a mistake. He boarded the wrong train from Holborn and found himself on the short dead-end to Aldwych. His follower of the moment dived for a phone-box and then waited to see whether Leo doubled back.

But Leo decided to surface again. He emerged into the lights and drizzle of the Strand just as a purple Mercedes, looking black under the street-lights, coasted to an illegal halt with the nearer back door already opening.

'Get in, Leo.'

Seeing a half-familiar face, Leo squeezed his big bulk inside. The big car re-entered the traffic. Twisting his head round, Leo could see no sign of followers. He relaxed in the soft seat but only to the extent that his weight was evenly spread. His muscles remained taut. He was remembering that the Filbustini brothers had never been among his favourite people.

'Thanks, Pepe,' he said gruffly. 'Drop me anywhere, I can manage from here.'

Pepe Filbustini, on his right, produced a grin which changed oddly in the shifting light. 'Just drive around for a while, Mark, while we have a little talk,' he said and his brother at the wheel headed for Waterloo Bridge. The brothers resembled each other, squat but strong and with faces which could have come out of the mould of the Hollywood badman, craggy and yet handsome, modelled by a heavy hand. As was only to be expected, the front passenger seat was occupied by a young blonde who sparkled in the glare of oncoming headlamps.

Leo sighed. He might have expected something like this. But he could cope. 'Drop the bird off, then,' he said. 'Not that I've anything to say.'

'Sorry, Leo,' Pepe said. 'We forgot that you and women don't get along. But she stays, just in case we want a witness that we've never seen or heard of you.' There was a pistol in his hand now and he let Leo see it.

Leo saw it and again he nearly smiled. Two near-smiles in one day was, for him, something of a record. Although not given to carrying firearms, Leo was well acquainted with them. Trust Pepe Filbustini, he thought, to play at James Bond with a Walther PPK. The external hammer might make it safe to carry with the hammer down, but it also made it very vulnerable at close quarters. The indicator pin showed that there was a cartridge in the chamber, so the gun was no empty bluff.

'If you want trouble,' Leo said softly, 'this is my day for handing it out.'

The girl in the front seat hunched down. Just her luck, to find herself in a car with perhaps the three hardest men in London and trouble about to explode.

But Pepe, when he spoke, was pacific. 'No trouble, Leo. We're not even going to ask you where Maurice's planted. We're here to help you.'

'I can manage without your help.'

'You can manage a damn sight better with it. If you were going to be met, they've let you down. You'll have the fuzz and every thug in the country looking for you. You'll never be able to enjoy your money until you get it out of the country. Right? Or has the money already gone out for real?'

'Tony Hayes was working for you, was he?' Leo said. 'I put him down as trying to make a deal with the law.'

'He was working for both.'

'So what are you offering?' Leo grunted. 'And how much would it cost?'

'For thirty grand, cash up front, you get board and lodgings for a month while the heat goes off and you can grow a beard. Then a change of appearance, new clothes, a passport, ticket to Spain, your money in a Barcelona bank and the use of a villa for the first six months. That should see you all right?'

'Yeah,' Leo said. 'For thirty grand.'

'Peanuts,' Pepe said. 'Against what you got salted away, that's only ten per cent plus expenses. Cheap at the price. If you still got the money, that is.'

Leo thought it over. He was under no delusions as to his chances if he accepted the deal. 'Back over the river,' he said suddenly. 'I've still got the money. That was just a story for Hayes' benefit. Head out Mile End Road.'

'I always knew you had sense,' Pepe said. 'Where are we going?'

'Hackney Marshes. I got a tin trunk buried in one of the recreation grounds.' There were seven or eight recreation grounds around Hackney Marshes, or had been when Leo went inside. The vaguer the directions, for the moment, the safer he would be. 'We'll need a spade.'

'We got one in the boot,' Mark said over his shoulder. Leo nodded to himself. There would certainly be a spade in the boot.

Mark Filbustini was a competent driver. They made good time. They approached Hackney Marshes by way of Victoria Park Road. Leo began to feign uncertainty. They circled the area until he had selected a suitably lonely spot. 'Pull off to the right here,' he said.

The car swung off, bobbed for a few seconds and then settled down to crawl slowly over grass.

For a rough-house with guns involved, Leo preferred close quarters such as the inside of a car. It was dark, but he had already taken his bearings and the light from the dashboard would be enough. He began his move by pointing across his own body and Pepe's with his left hand. 'It's over there,' he said.

As both men looked to the right Leo brought his left hand down on the Walther, his thumb preventing any movement of the hammer. He tried not to think of the small ridge of metal in the mechanism, which was all that stood between him and one hell of a bang. He used his right elbow and all his strength in a backward blow to the body. Pepe was well-muscled but the wind came out of him in a hoot like a fog-horn and he folded over. The Walther came away, bringing some skin with it.

The car was stopped and Mark Filbustini was grabbing at his waistband. Leo punched him behind the ear, throwing him forward to the accompaniment of a blare on the horns.

The interior lights came on. Leo switched the pistol to his right hand and grabbed the girl by the hair with his left before she could complete her exit.

'Everybody be good and nobody gets hurt any more,' he said. His audience now comprised two groaners and a weeper but his words seemed to be getting through. 'You, darling.' He gave the girl's hair a jerk. His mother's voice seemed to be protesting in his ears but with the adrenalin flowing he hardly heard it. 'Put your hand down Mark's front – I dare say it's been there before – and pull out his gun. Handle it carefully once it's out, until then I don't mind. Pass it back to me. And your handbag,' he added. The Filbustinis' women were as likely to be armed as the men.

With Mark Filbustini's gun – also a Walther – safely in his pocket, Leo began to relax. 'Now,' he said, 'I'll tell you what we're going to do. Listen carefully, because if anybody tries anything there's going to be a lot of death around here. We're going to get out. Mark first. When he's standing where I can see him, with his hands on the bonnet, Pepe and I will get out together. And then you, darling. If one of you runs, the other two get it.'

Pepe's breath was coming back. He half-straightened. 'Your days are numbered, Leo,' he said.

'Don't threaten,' Leo said. 'At the moment, all I want is a head start. Threaten me and I might start you digging graves. You were going to forget about Maurie and send me abroad? Like fuck you were.' That, and the conviction in Leo's voice, put a halt to further argument.

When he had the three of them ranged against the side of the car, nicely silhouetted against the lights, Leo said, 'Now, clothes off and throw them into the car. Every stitch. All of you.'

This was too much. Mark span round. 'See here, you sodding—'

He was stopped by a kick to the kneecap which put him down, sobbing. His brother began to move but saw, even in the faint light, that the barrel of his own gun was centred between his eyes.

'Last one into the buff gets another of the same,' Leo said. 'I'm going to leave you with one ten-pee coin between you. You can toss it to see who goes to look for a lonely phone-box.'

'And guess who's going to lose,' the girl said bitterly. Her accent would not have disgraced a princess of royal blood.

FOUR

Maud Venable still worked as a clerkess in the shipping office where Leo had first known her. The first impression which she made was one of thinness. Her physique was thin, her voice was thin and even her black-tinted hair was thinning. The second impression was one of extreme timidity.

Leo and Maud had enjoyed – insofar as Maud could be said to enjoy anything – a relationship lasting many years. They suited each other well. Maud was nervously grateful to be noticed, embraced and subsidised by any man, while Leo had obtained the comfort of the one woman in the world who was obviously and completely unthreatening. It was a relationship as near to love as either of them was capable of sustaining.

The night was advanced before Leo reached the vicinity of Maud's flat in Stepney. Leo had been busy. He had disposed of the clothing into the canal but had retained the girl's trinkets and jewellery for Maud, adding the money from the Filbustinis' wallets to his own hoard. The Mercedes he had abandoned where he thought that it would cause most inconvenience to the early morning traffic.

He had then spent some time in a public lavatory,

making sure that his clothing contained no electronic signalling devices, after which he had set off on a journey circuitous enough to have thrown off any possibility of pursuit. He made his final approach through a series of alleys, in case the roving police or anyone else were still on the lookout for a glimpse of him. He had phoned Maud from a call-box and the door was off the latch. He looked around for watchers and then, satisfied, slipped in through the shadows.

She met him in the hall and stood, passive, while he sampled the vibrations. But all was well. 'Nobody knows about us, still?' he asked.

'Not from me,' she said.

'Nor me neither.' Only then did he relax and give her a peck on the cheek. 'How you been, then?'

'OK. And you?'

'Well as could be expected. I kept myself fit, best I could. I couldn't write or send you any money.'

'I understood that, Leo. I managed up to now. But they say the area's going to be redeveloped and they want me out of the flat.'

'That's too bad,' he said. 'You still got that envelope?'

'Quite safe.' It was under the carpet in the middle of the bedroom floor. It took them twenty minutes of furniture-shifting to recover it.

When he had his cheques, passbook and a set of convincing identity documents in his hands, he glanced into her wardrobe. His things were still there – two suits which should still fit him and a variety of small props for changing his appearance. Leo relaxed and put an arm round her skinny frame.

'Thank God that's all safe!' he said. 'These papers are the only link with my money. I'll go to the bank in the morning. Then, a visit to the races, just to make an explanation if anyone ever wonders where a roll of notes came from. And we'll find you another place, a better one. After that ... I'll need to get abroad. Somewhere peaceful and sunny. You want to come with me?'

'You don't need me along,' she said. 'Get yourself a younger bit of stuff.'

'You'll do for me,' he said gruffly.

'Oh Leo!' She sniffed and then tried, not very hard, to slip out of his grasp. 'It's good to have you back. When did you have a meal? You'll be needing something to eat.'

He gripped until her ribs creaked. 'There's something I need which I haven't had for a damn sight longer than my last meal. We can think about food afterwards.'

In the morning, he left her hobbling painfully around the flat. She had phoned her office and pleaded illness, which was not far from the truth. Leo was not a considerate lover and his great weight had been almost too much for her. She was not getting any younger.

The branch bank stood as he remembered it, the one fixed point in the shifting scene of a busy shopping street. Even the cashier was the same man although older. Leo had resumed the disguise which he had worn in the past, no more than a walrus moustache, a hat, a dark overcoat, horn-rimmed spectacles and a limp accentuated by the use of a stick, and he thought the man half-recognised him.

He gave his account number, which had burned into his memory over the years, and showed the cashier his cheque-book. 'I'll want to transfer some money,' he said carefully. The bank had been used to a better-spoken version of himself. 'Could I have a note of the balance?'

'Certainly.' The cashier retired behind a screen. He

36

returned within a minute and handed over a folded slip. 'And how are things in Hong Kong?' he asked.

Leo remembered in time the supposed provenance of the account. 'Unsettled,' he said, glancing at the slip.

£1,382.54, it said.

It took a moment for the unfamiliar decimals to register. Then he stood still.

'Is something wrong?' the cashier asked.

A warning voice told him to do nothing which might be remembered. 'I thought there was a larger balance,' he said mildly.

'I'll check again.' The cashier went back to the computer terminal. He returned looking mildly worried. 'There seems to have been a substantial withdrawal within the last few weeks, but I can't seem to get any details. These damned computers . . .'

Leo breathed again. 'A computer error?' he suggested.

But the cashier shook his head. 'Oh no.' He leaned closer and lowered his voice. 'We do get the occasional error, but it's human error. Sometimes money goes into the wrong account, because that depends on somebody reading the name correctly and finding the account of the right Joe Bloggs. But I've never known a case of the money coming out of the wrong account. Never. You see, it's done by the computer reading the magnetised numbers on a cheque or a card. There's been a genuine withdrawal. We could investigate . . .'

Leo managed a laugh. 'My partner must have made the transfer,' he said. 'I thought he wanted me to do it. That man could make a crisis out of having a pee. Well, while I'm here I may as well draw some cash.'

He hurried back to the flat, almost forgetting to lean on his stick. Blood pounded in his head and he felt his stomach churning.

It had been Maud Venable's good luck to be the one woman with whom Leo felt safe. It had enabled her to hold her lover when the passing years would otherwise have driven him in search of younger meat. But now it was to be her dire misfortune. Leo would never have dared to treat any other woman as he now treated Maud.

When Leo returned to the flat with a gleam in his eye and, without a word, began to strip her, she thought that the night's passion was on him again and braced herself for more incursions into her still tender flesh. Even when Leo, with unfeeling efficiency, had produced a length of sash-cord and tied her wrists behind her, she did not struggle. Leo had been known to assert his dominance in that way.

But instead of kneeling her by the couch, Leo passed the end of the cord over the top hinge of the living-room door and down to the further handle, pulling her up until only her toes reached the carpet. He had taped her lips together on the left side of her mouth. She could still speak, after a fashion, out of the other corner but if she had dared to scream the sound would not have reached her neighbours.

An hour later, her skinny body was covered, front and back, with welts from his stick and there had been other, more painful indignities. But the time for violence was past. Leo was seated facing her.

'It has to be you,' he said for the tenth time. 'Nobody else could have got access to my account. And a hundred and fifty grand doesn't just get up and walk.'

She shook her head violently. Strands of hair swung and adhered to her wet cheeks. She made a noise, strangled by the tape and her sobs.

'If you've something to say, say it.' He gave her a half-hearted tap with the stick, just as a reminder.

She struggled for control and at last managed to articulate a word which he interpreted as 'Police'.

'Have they been at you?' he asked sharply.

She shook her head again.

'Well then. No way could they have found that account and been sure it was mine, unless you let them in on it.'

Again the headshake. She tried to speak again. Leo cut more tape. 'Speak up,' he said. 'Last chance.'

Listening carefully, he thought that she was trying to say something about the computer and a mistake.

'The man at the bank said not, but of course he would say that.'

He got up to seal her mouth altogether. 'You've nothing left to say.' He sat for a few minutes, deep in thought, before he spoke again. 'Here's how I see it. There's four or five ways it could've happened. You got together with somebody cleverer to fix it.'

She tried to tell him with her eyes that this was wrong.

'Or somebody in the bank saw that the account was lying idle and tried a bit of embezzlement for himself. Or, what you said, the fuzz got on to the account and put some sort of a stopper on it. OK, so you agree,' he said in response to her frantic nodding. 'You could be right. But if that's the case why wasn't I arrested? They've lost the chance now, because I drew most of the balance in cash. Or the bloke in the bank was wrong. Maybe the computer blew a gasket. But how do I get it put right without drawing attention? What I need's a bent bank-clerk who can tell me how these things work.'

She wanted to point out that he was not the only one capable of a fraud, but she could only make noises through her nose.

He paused and studied her abject form. 'None of this does you any good, old girl. I couldn't trust you again after this. You've had your time. I'm sorry,' he added. The voices of his mother and sisters were loud in his ears.

He left her hanging there while he packed his things and wiped his fingerprints off everything which he could remember touching. He even slacked off the cord so that her heels could take her weight, for he was not a sadist.

He thought that he could snuff her out without a qualm, but when the time came he heard again those voices from the past. She pleaded with her eyes, even turned, trying to tempt him with her body. He turned suddenly, gathered his bags and left the flat.

FIVE

The Chief Executive of the National Bank was not a man of formidable appearance, being small, balding and close to retirement age. In the expensive dignity of his private office, he looked almost an intruder. But he bristled with energy and such were his power and his ruthlessness that, when he frowned, strong men and even Treasury officials blenched. He was frowning now, and Vernon Boforth, who was noted for his talents rather than his strength, was blenching as he had never blenched before.

God was not thundering, indeed he seemed to be speaking with unusual gentleness, but Vernon had not been invited to sit down, which was a mark of grave displeasure.

'So it would seem,' said God, 'that we have here a combination of circumstances which might not be significant on their own but which, taken together, give cause for concern. We have a depositor who seemed surprised at the modest size of his balance. He passed it off as having been an unexpected transfer by his partner, but there are no other authorised signatories to that account. And there has been a transaction about which your computer seems to have developed almost total amnesia. The balance shown in that account has been reduced by a hundred and fifty thousand pounds without any record of a withdrawal excepting only the date on which the balance changed, now two weeks old, against a blank line in the statement. Very sensibly, the cashier made a report to his manager, who passed it onward. Could it be accounted for by an attack of hiccups on the part of your machine?'

Vernon Boforth fidgeted from foot to foot and tried not to speak as a small boy might address the headmaster. He would dearly have loved to give an affirmative answer, but in the face of assurances which he had given in the past he did not dare. 'Very unlikely,' he said. 'The computer's programmed to throw up any such malfunctions so that they can be dealt with immediately. There have been very few, but the fail-safe system has always worked.'

'That would seem to suggest an act of fraud. I understood that the computer was tamper-proof.'

Boforth began to sweat, but he kept his voice under control and chose his words carefully. 'If you look back to my original reports,' he said, 'you'll see that I made it clear that any code man can make, man can break. In fact I advised, on the basis of American experience, that a budget be set aside each year to cover any possible losses. I pointed out that a budgetary figure of even half a million a year would have been more than offset by the administrative savings. Every feasible encryption or coding for its protection was incorporated, but there's a limit. Any more, and the system would have been too cumbersome to operate.'

'I could believe,' God said slowly, 'that the depositor was either deluded or fraudulent, except that we have a gap in the computer records of the very same transaction. So we are left with staff error, computer error or fraud. Which is it?'

'It can't be anything but fraud,' Boforth said reluctantly. Blaming the computer would have caused fewer waves but he could not bring himself to do it. The computer program had been his baby.

'I understand,' God said, 'that the totals for the period are in balance. If there was a fraud, therefore, it involved a transfer between two accounts within this bank. Could the computer be employed to search for an account which gained a deposit of just that amount?'

Boforth looked up at the ornate ceiling. 'Very easily,' he said at last. 'But it would be pointless.'

'And why, may I ask?'

'Because computer fraud requires education, expertise, sophistication. It isn't committed by your neighbourhood yob. Nobody who was capable of tampering with the computer would be naïve enough to make a single deposit elsewhere. They would open more than one temporary account, transfer the money in smaller sums over a period, adding or subtracting a sum to obscure the total, then bring the money together at its destination, probably lay a dozen or more false trails, close the temporary accounts and expunge them from the records. We'd be looking for accounts whose transactions over an unknown period included an unknown number which added up to a hundred and fifty thousand, give or take an unknown amount. And then we'd have to check the validity of every such transfer. It would amount almost to a Total Audit.'

God shook his head. 'A Total Audit costs almost as much as the amount in question. And, after all, we haven't had a complaint as yet. If – and I stress the "if" – there had been a fraud, would bank staff be involved?'

'Not necessarily,' Boforth said. 'The system's designed so that staff know little more than the man in the street. Of course, if one of the bank's terminals was used we could find that out. All their transactions are automatically recorded on magnetic tape.'

'Do that. And staff are obliged to open their personal accounts for examination. It's a forlorn hope, but you'd better go through them. If that doesn't produce answers, you'll have to look further afield.'

'Me?' Boforth said, startled.

'Who else?' God's eyebrows rose at the naïvety of the man. 'You did the original program. And you did a good job,' he added, his fairness tempered with condescension. 'In five years, this is the first sign of a breach. Compared to our friends in the States, we're getting off lightly. I hear that they have computer fraud the way we have electronic games. Anyway, as part of your contract for that work, you now head the Computer Department. But, whatever your strengths may be, you're not really a manager.'

'I'm not really a detective either.'

God pretended not to hear the impertinence but filed it away for later retribution. He had opposed the appointment of this brilliant but unstable man and had been over-ruled. 'Your deputy does all the real administration; your value lies in your understanding of the software. If anybody has managed to – what is that extraordinary expression?'

'Hack in.'

' – to hack into our system, I want to know. But I want it confidential. So we'll keep this in-house for the moment and you're the obvious man to do the investigation. So get on with it. Take what help you want – I suggest that new man, Hancock; he seems to have been sired by a microchip.

'If you can't find any explanation internally, you'll have to go outside.'

'I don't quite understand, sir,' Boforth said.

'Must I spell it out?' God demanded irritably. 'Or write a program? How many places in the country do they have a compatible computer, together with the expertise for this sort of tampering? As it happens, I do remember your original reports, and one of the reasons you gave for the choice of this particular hardware was the individuality of the system and the comparative paucity of compatible computers.

'So go to the manufacturers for a list of users. Visit them. Look for contacts with our members of staff. Look for sudden affluence. Anything suspicious, you phone in for a check of the bank-balance of that individual or body. I want detailed, regular reports. If and when, but not until, you get something solid, you bring in the police. Is that clear?'

'Absolutely,' said Boforth.

'Of course, you may not get anything. But, in the event of there being a loophole, I want to be able to show the board that we did everything possible.'

Boforth looked happier. This had the makings of a good swan-off. He made a mental note to take along his golf clubs. With a little luck, a supply of contraceptives might turn out to be a wise provision.

SIX

It was the turn of Polly Holt and Peter Helinger to walk through the busy quadrangles. Students preparing for their degree examinations scurried from building to building with worried expressions. Helinger looked as harassed as any of them. Polly, although she could only guess at the reason for the meeting, looked scared out of her wits.

Dr Westerly joined them in his small retiring room. 'Mrs Whatsit gave me your message,' he said. 'Do sit down. What's the panic?'

'I don't feel like sitting,' Helinger said, but he dropped loosely into one of the padded chairs. 'I had a phone-call from a friend at one of the technical colleges. Apparently Polly's friend Boforth, the man who programmed the computer at the National Bank, just paid him a two-day visit and subjected him to a gentle sort of inquisition. And then I opened the mail and found a letter from Boforth, demanding an appointment next week.'

'Why did he phone you?' Polly asked. 'Does he think— ?'

'Just a friendly gossip,' Helinger said.

'I bet! Oh God!' Polly said. 'I knew I shouldn't have

had anything to do with it. Now everybody knows.'

'Nobody knows anything,' Westerly said. 'Calm yourself. And the phone-call isn't significant. What bothers me is that Boforth's heading this way at all. Surely there must be too many computers in the country for this sort of investigation to be worth his while?'

'Not so many mainframes which would be compatible over a telephone-link,' Helinger said. He ran his fingers through his hair in a nervous gesture which left it standing erect in apparent fear. 'The bank went for a system with a high baud rate, far higher than domestic micros but on a par with educational use. Industrial applications are usually purpose-designed . . .' His voice trailed away.

'Come down out of the clouds,' Westerly said, 'and explain what the hell you're talking about.'

'If he went to the manufacturers and asked for a list of customers who've got compatible mainframes, I'd guess – and I'm only guessing – that the list wouldn't run to more than forty or fifty names, mostly educational but a few commercial.'

'If you'd told us that,' Polly said miserably, hanging her head, 'I'd never have let you involve me.'

'How was I to know you were clueless?' Helinger retorted. 'And in your own field, too.'

'Cool down, both of you,' Westerly said. 'You're acting as if retribution was knocking at the door. In point of fact, Polly, if you've destroyed your notes and re-formatted your discs as I suggested – you have done that, haven't you?' he asked sharply.

Polly nodded without looking up.

'Then there's no evidence pointing towards us at all. As long as none of us admits anything, we're bomb-proof.'

'There's all the time I spent on the computer,' Polly said. 'If he hangs around long enough asking questions, somebody'll remember that.'

'If he's around that long,' Helinger said, 'he'll wonder about the unusual lack of redundancies, and somebody'll mention the benefaction – which they aren't supposed to know about, but it's common knowledge.'

'Only a rumour,' Westerly corrected. 'I spread it myself. Confidentiality was a prime condition of the benefaction. If he asks a direct question, the University authorities will deny it and point to the Vice Chancellor's fund-raising activities. All the same, it might be better if he were defused. Polly, tell us about Boforth. You used to know him.'

'I saw him around, that's all.'

'You'd have heard all about him.'

Polly sighed. 'If it'll help, although I don't see how. Vernon Boforth's a bit of a genius at computing. Honestly, he's out of my class. Things I have to work out, he knows without thinking about them.'

'Our more brilliant colleagues tend to be unstable outside of their specialities,' Westerly said. 'It may be heresy to say this within these portals, where it's a matter of faith that because a man is the world's foremost expert on electron spin resonance he must be God's gift to management, but most of them are babes in arms, quite unfit to face the real world. Does Boforth fit into that category?'

'Not by a mile. Crisp and businesslike, seen from a distance.' Given something to think about, Polly calmed down. 'I did hear—'

'Yes?'

'Oh, just one or two stories which suggested that he couldn't take pressure.'

'I see,' Westerly said. 'Go on. Describe him.'

'What's to describe? Very much a confirmed bachelor. Tall. Brown hair. A nice smile. Apart from a certain weakness about the mouth and chin I suppose he's good-looking,' Polly said thoughtfully, never having considered the matter. 'And doesn't he half know it! A bum-pincher.'

'Only a bum-pincher? Or a fully-fledged lecher?' Westerly asked sharply.

'A lecher. No doubt of it. No steady girl-friend, but he had it away with every girl in the place.' She realised that the two men were looking at her curiously. 'I'm not a girl, I'm a mathematician,' she said firmly. 'He never tried it on with me.'

'Perhaps that's his Achilles' heel,' Helinger said suddenly. 'We could get one of the better-looking typists to . . .distract him.'

'To sleep with him, you mean,' Polly said. 'You don't have to be mealy-mouthed with me. I may not be a swinger but I did Biology and I know about the birds and the bees.' She stopped and produced an unexpectedly wicked grin which made both men blink. 'I'll tell you something else I remember. If you want to make him run to the other end of the country, put him with some innocent-seeming young kid and tell her to ask him, afterwards, when he's going to marry her. He'd be over the horizon before you could blink.'

'I like your thinking,' Westerly said. 'But we can't risk bringing another person in on this.'

'In that case—'

'You'll have to do it.'

'Me?' Polly's voice went up to a squeak. She might know about the birds and the bees but, living an almost wholly cerebral life, she was only vaguely aware of having a body at all. She played no games and joined in no sports except occasionally to sail because the

49

mathematical intricacies of tidal navigation pleased her convoluted mind. 'I couldn't do it. And, anyway, he'd never look at me.'

'If we aren't careful, he's going to look damned hard at you,' Westerly said. 'Will he recognise you?'

'He might.'

'I should think it's a certainty,' Helinger said. 'Think about it. He comes here, looking for somebody who's driven a coach and horses through his precious encryptions, and sees a female scarecrow with goggles on whom he last saw at Cambridge while he was designing the system. And now look at it the other way round. If you had your hair styled and tinted, and contact lenses instead of those hideous glasses, and if you were dressed in feminine clothes which actually fitted you instead of having been bought in jumble sales, and shoes with heels in place of those sandals, then would he recognise you?'

'In that unlikely eventuality, *I* wouldn't recognise me. I won't do it.'

Peter Helinger spoke gently. 'I hope you don't mind my asking but . . . have you ever . . . ?'

As far as Polly was concerned, the subject was unimportant and therefore discussable. 'You mean, am I a sexual virgin? Or do I have an intact hymen? Yes to the first, probably not to the second. I don't set any great store by my virginal state, but I'm not enamoured of the idea of being christened by Vernon Blasted Boforth and becoming a pubic scalp on his belt.'

'You needn't sleep with him if you don't want to,' Westerly said generously. 'Just so long as you distract him and prevent him remembering that you used to work in his field.'

'Gee, thanks,' Polly said. 'Anyway, he likes his meat rare. He'd as soon make a pass at your Mrs Whatsit. Her

50

name's Blyth, by the way.'

Dr Westerly was shaking his head. 'You've never really looked at yourself,' he said. 'Under those Oxfam rejects you've got a nice figure, and your features are good. You'll be amazed when you see yourself. You could make heads turn.'

'I don't particularly want to turn heads,' Polly said irritably. 'And I'm not going out shopping for girlish things. I'd feel stupid. And I wouldn't know what to get.'

'Of course not,' Westerly said. 'You'd only come back looking like a tidier version of the same scruffy object we've come to know. One of us will have to go with you and steer you firmly away from the bargain basement.'

Polly had taken no offence and some of her objections seemed to have evaporated. 'Do you have to have me along at all?' she asked with a sigh indicative of great patience. 'It seems an awful waste of valuable academic time. If you two fancy yourselves as Svengalis or fairy godmothers or whatever, couldn't you just buy something for me?'

'You'll have to try things on,' Helinger said with equal patience. 'And neither of us can have your hair done for you. Also, there's a cosmetic consultant dishing out free advice in Hallingham's this week. Dr Westerly can go with you.'

Westerly jumped as if the chair had bitten him. 'No he bloody well can't,' he said. 'For all my years, I'm an engaged man; and although Joanna's abroad just now she'd soon hear about it if I started buying frilly things for pretty girls.'

'I'm not a—'

'You would be by the time I was finished with you. Peter, you'll have to do it.'

'Damned if I do. I'm in the throes of a divorce and if Pat got wind of me squiring a girl round the sort of shops I have in mind she'd screw me for a settlement which would clean me out.'

'Are you still speaking to Pat?' Westerly asked. 'Maybe she'd help if you asked her nicely. I've never seen her looking less than gorgeous, and if she's after you for support it wouldn't suit her book if you came a cropper and ended up on the dole or in the States.'

'We're still speaking,' Helinger said. 'In fact, she's speaking rather sweetly at the moment, because she's the one who wants the divorce and she feels guilty about it. And I'd like to keep it that way. You speak to her.'

'She'd think that I had a girl-friend,' Westerly protested. 'Apart from Joanna, I mean.'

'Would it matter? Joanna and she can't stand each other.'

'Which makes it all the more certain that the story would get back.'

'That's true,' Helinger admitted. 'All right. I'll ask her myself. I don't know how I'll put it or what she'll say, but I'll ask.'

'There's one thing you seem to have forgotten,' Polly said. 'Who's going to pay for all this?'

There was a short silence. It was a subject which both men had hoped to avoid. 'After all,' Westerly said at last, 'you get the long-term benefit.'

'By then the clothes will be sort of second-hand,' Polly pointed out. 'And I doubt whether I'll ever wear any of them again, once Vernon Boforth's moved on. Anyway, you're in this as deep as I am. I think you should each put in a third.'

'If I were mad enough to kick in a third,' Helinger said, 'I'd expect to end up with a third of the clothes, which wouldn't suit me, and a third of your hair-do, which is ridiculous. Ten per cent, that's my last word.'

'Twenty-five,' Polly said briskly. 'You each pay a quarter and I'll pay half. That seems fair.'

They settled down to negotiations.

Vernon Boforth's visit to the University was short but, for himself at least, sweet. He found himself the guest of charming companions who differed from those whom he had encountered at his earlier ports of call only in the degree of their willingness to entertain him to lunch or to join him on the golf-course. But he was unable to take full advantage of their hospitality, being distracted by the charms of a young demonstrator in the Computer Department, a shy but attractive brunette with a combination of gamine prettiness and an air of innocence which brought out the very devil in him.

He lusted. For two days he laid siege and by the third morning he was gone.

But while Boforth was engaged in silken – or at least nylon – dalliance, Edward Hancock was putting on what was at first no more than a show of activity. In his view, Boforth was overdue to come a cropper; and, if that should happen while they were working in harness, Hancock intended to be in a position to show that he at least had been diligent. A university, thronged with too many individuals to know each other by sight, and all with good reason to move from building to building, is the easiest place on earth for a stranger to penetrate. Hancock, looking more like a visiting lecturer than do most lecturers, wandered busily around with some papers in his hand to add protective colouration and fell into conversation whenever he pleased. His background made entry into the life of the Maths Building particularly easy. He spoke much, saying very little and listening and learning all the time.

Ted Hancock should have shown more understanding of Boforth, for he also had a high intelligence flawed. He had been born with a talent for the absorption of knowledge which could have carried him out of the ambit of his respectable but mediocre origins by way of almost any profession which he had cared to embrace. He had excelled in the New Mathematics and, embracing accountancy, had shone again. The universal application of the computer had found him still young and flexible enough in mind to master the new techniques which older colleagues seemed to find so baffling.

It was therefore not surprising that he had more than once been earmarked for the top; yet, each time, he had failed even to hold the job which he had. His trouble was drink, an inherited tendency towards alcoholism handed down from a grandfather and nurtured by a pair of convivial uncles. His alcoholism was subject to periodic cycles of many months or even of a year or more. He would plumb the depths. Delirium tremens was no more than a familiar evil. Then, when money ran short or death from alcoholic poisoning began to loom, he would sign himself into a clinic where he was known and even trusted. Dried out and determined, he would return to the outside world a total abstainer and would, with little difficulty, find another responsible job, pay off the clinic and even lay the foundation for a modest nest-egg. After weeks or months firmly ensconced on the wagon, he would feel confident enough to become a mild, social drinker. Even this phase might endure for a long period. But, sooner or later, the balance would tip and he would be off again down the slippery slope.

The balance was tipping now and it was the University which finally weighted it against him. The department head, finding a presentable and knowledgeable stranger in his midst, had carried him off to the Staff Club for cocktails and a vinous lunch and, being himself a lover of the grape, had dispensed with a heavy hand well into the afternoon.

The professor was a garrulous man, and the wine and the presence of an interested stranger for audience loosened his tongue. It took only an occasional question to keep him chatting about his staff and their doings.

When they parted, Ted Hancock was nodding to himself. Only his closest associates would have recognised the signs, but the doom was on him again.

Pat Helinger had come to the aid of her estranged husband's little friend without asking more than a dozen or so questions, and had used her remarkable sense of style to good effect. She had been suspicious at first, until it had been explained that the motherless Polly was shortly to be married to a childhood sweetheart who was on the point of returning from Canada and would expect to find an adult version of the same attractive girl whom he had last seen in school uniform.

Polly went along with the fiction with an air of amused tolerance, but had soon been caught up in the novelty of her new image. The illusion, which came from wearing light clothes and featherweight lingerie, of being naked from the waist down, she found shocking but, once she had become used to the cold, euphoric.

Around the University, Polly's transmogrification had been no more than a passing wonder. Many of her colleagues were as unworldly as herself and their reactions had ranged from a vague comment that she seemed to have done something to her hair to blank lack of recognition coupled with a feeling that it would be pleasant to have a decent-looking girl around the place for a change and curiosity as to who had managed to get authority for extra staff in time of crisis.

When Boforth had made hasty farewells and had departed in the direction of East Anglia, taking a strangely reticent Hancock with him, Doctors Westerly and Helinger descended into the bowels of the Maths Building to seek out Polly in her lair. This was a large but gloomy cavern, half filled with metal racking and stacked with boxes of discs, magnetic or paper tape, punched cards and ream upon ream of paper, punched, printed or scribbled.

The new Polly Holt was seated at the trestle table which served her as a desk, working on a large, critical path diagram in a space which had been cleared by raising higher the stacks of paper around the table's perimeter. She had confined her makeup to a touch of lipstick and her hair had received only perfunctory attention from a hairbrush, but fortunately the hairdresser had chosen a casual style and her skin was good. She had not, after all, reverted to her earlier style of dress. She looked up and nodded vaguely at Helinger.

'There you are,' she said. 'At last. I need help. I've got a problem.'

'Problem?' Helinger said. 'Is it bad?'

'This program of Jorkins. It seems to give the computer the collywobbles and I can't see any reason. I've tried—'

Westerly laughed and Peter Helinger held up his hand in a traffic-stopping gesture until her voice trailed away. 'Blast your program,' he said. 'Tell us what happened.'

'Happened?'

'With Boforth.'

'Who?'

'For Heaven's sake don't be coy!' Helinger said irritably.

'Cool down,' Westerly said. 'She isn't being coy, she's just away in a world of her own. Polly, we're speaking of the charming, well-dressed and not unhandsome man who heaped you with flowers and carried you off to dinner last night.'

'Oh, him.' Polly put down her pencil and concentrated. Her anxious expression was replaced by the shadow of a complacent smile. 'I got rid of him for you.'

'What happened?' Westerly asked before he could stop himself. 'I mean, how?'

'Pretty much what you'd expect, I suppose,' Polly said thoughtfully, 'although I don't know much about these things. I tarted myself up until I felt like somebody's Christmas present and he carted me off to dinner at the Oaken Tree.'

'That's pricey,' Helinger said, impressed.

'I dare say he charged it to expenses,' Polly said. 'Actually, it was a nice change not being expected to go Dutch. He plied me with wines, which was another nice change although I managed to keep a clear head. At least I think I did. We went on to a nightclub sort of place to dance. He's a good dancer. I hadn't danced for years, but my mother insisted on my taking lessons when I was a child. In those days, I thought it a terrible waste of time but I don't suppose that any form of learning is ever really wasted.'

'This isn't exactly what we wanted to know,' Westerly said gently.

'I suppose not. Well, he'd tried to pump me over dinner and I'd let him see that I didn't have the faintest idea what he was talking about, so as far as he's concerned we're still whiter than white. Anyway, he was much more interested in trying to get to grips with me.

57

'Then, this morning, just as I suggested to you, I made nestbuilding noises and there was a yelp and a sort of whooshing sound and he was gone. I'm exaggerating, you understand?' she added. 'But not very much.'

'We gathered that,' Westerly said. 'Er – where did the farewell scene take place?'

She met his eye. 'This morning, over breakfast in his hotel room.'

Dr Westerly had turned faintly pink. 'My dear child!' he said. 'We certainly didn't mean it to come to this.'

'I didn't either,' Polly said cheerfully. 'Perhaps it was the wine after all. But I can't honestly say that I feel violated, or deflowered, or anything like that. I think that he must have been very good at it. Very gentle and all that. And I never knew that satisfying the biological urges could be quite such fun. I think I'll have to find myself a lover, or possibly even a husband.'

Dr Helinger, mindful of his imminent divorce, made a strangled sound in his throat. Westerly, safer in his engaged state, looked politely interested.

'While I remember,' Polly said, 'here are the credit-card chits for the clothes and things. You'd better square up with me before the bill comes in or my cheque'll bounce.'

Westerly ran his eyes over the scraps of paper and arrived at a rough total. 'Good God!' he said. 'Did you get ten of everything? If you were stocking your bottom drawer for this projected husband you mentioned, I don't feel obliged to contribute.'

Polly looked abashed but defiant. 'You told me to get the best,' she pointed out. 'I know it seems all wrong to pay fifty quid for a pair of camiknicks you could pull through a wedding-ring—' the wicked grin suddenly transformed her gentle face '—but look at it this way. You made Vernon Boforth very happy.'

SEVEN

Harry Moyes was another of those men of flawed talent, with whom the upper reaches of the world of crime are populated. His talent was financial and his flaw was a simple inability to remain honest. Like Kipling's Jew he could sense the ebb and flow of money, predict its vagaries and understand the forces which moved it. He even looked the part, sleek, portly and prosperous with silver hair and a tongue to match. Not to trust him required a suspension of faith.

Harry could have been honestly prosperous, even rich, but the pickings, although smaller, were easier for a professional bankrupt. His chosen field was the building industry. He knew little or nothing about building – what little work was actually undertaken he left to his partner – but he knew how to make it pay. It was his habit to establish, within easy reach of London, a potentially legitimate business in one of building's byways such as double glazing, cavity insulation, concrete paving or low-cost central heating. Like Harry himself, each business could have flourished, safely and in its own right. But that would have smacked of honest toil, and somewhere in Harry's psyche lurked a preference for double dealing.

So Harry would build up the business, complete with brochures and testimonials from satisfied if fictitious customers, until a satisfactory load of debts, to suppliers and to any clients rash enough to have deposited money in advance, loomed over it. When the pricking of his thumbs told him that the moment was right the assets would vanish inconspicuously, their absence being accounted for by carefully-presented paperwork, and there would be another liquidation followed by another move, another name and a fresh start.

Creditors might threaten and pursue, but the loopholes in the law were so familiar to Harry Moyes that it seemed as if the game might go on for ever. And it might well have done so but for a single, unfortunate slip. Usually, Harry or his staff checked out each prospective victim, just to be sure that they had no legal or political clout; but the contract for re-windowing a whole street of flats was so remunerative, and the deposit so promptly paid, that the status of the client as a young widow seemed to be recommendation enough.

But the young widow had been the sister of the Filbustini brothers, property barons and at that time two of the hardest men around the Smoke. They followed the time-honoured practices of the trade, buying up flats and houses in areas which were on the decline, evicting the sitting tenants with a ruthlessness reminiscent of a chicken-farmer putting a hen off its nest and replacing them with immigrants or prostitutes, depending on the status of the district, until such time as rehabilitation and disposal could be undertaken on a profitable scale.

When Harry learned the true identity of his clients he came close to a heart-attack. Through a friend, he offered to refund the deposit, but the Filbustinis would settle for nothing less than the completion of the contract. Harry could have found the deposit money, although not without difficulty because his former associates had already had their shares and, having also had word of the Filbustinis' unreasonable attitude, were lying very low. To complete the contract was quite beyond his means. It had been obtained on quoted prices which were impossibly low, although quite reasonable for a contract which Harry had never intended to fulfil. They were in fact less than the cost of purchasing the windows from the manufacturer and allowed nothing for the considerable costs of fitting and installation.

Faced with unacceptable options – to face the music or to complete the contract – Harry found a third. He ran for it, taking with him only Walter Pratt, his partner and right-hand-man. Walter it was who organised such practical work as was ever done in their ephemeral businesses.

The influence of the Filbustini brothers extended through the South of England, so the two headed into the Midlands. They settled in one of the smaller towns of the conurbation and rented office accommodation in a Portacabin on otherwise derelict ground. This time it was to be tarmacadam paths and drives.

After a few days, they met in Harry's office. This contained only one comfortable chair and Harry was in it. Walter perched on a corner of the desk, pushing aside a gin-bottle to make room for his skinny backside. Walter was, as usual, roughly dressed. He would have preferred to emulate Harry's elegance but it was a matter of policy that one of them should look as though he did some occasional building work. Besides, it saved money. The air was thick with old cigar-smoke.

'I took eight deposits,' Walter said.

'Fine,' said Harry. 'That makes thirteen.' He poured a

couple of drinks and opened a bottle of tonic.

'Unlucky number.'

'I don't know. It's a start. There aren't too many driveways around here, and most of the owners don't mind weeding their gravel. Maybe we should make a switch. Cheers!'

Walter lifted his glass. 'Cheers! We can't go back to windows,' he said. 'They'll be watching for that.'

'Solar heating?'

'In this climate?'

Harry looked out at the steady drizzle. 'You have a point there. For the moment, we'll just have to make this one pay off. What sort of rates did you get?'

'Not good,' Walter said. 'Contractors won't quote on our spec. They say it'll break up, first time there's a frost.'

'That's hardly any skin off their great, hairy noses,' Harry said indignantly. 'We're the ones giving the guarantees. Did they but know it, they'll have the chance of quoting for doing them again properly.' He took a pull at his drink, lit a fresh cigar and did some figuring on the back of an unpaid invoice. 'Another problem is that the VAT man is on to us already. At this rate we'll never hit the cut-off point. Not unless we buy the plant, hire the men and carry out some work ourselves.'

'We could go legit,' Walter said wistfully. 'It'd be nice to stay in one place for a while.'

'But not this place,' Harry said, with a reluctant glance through the clouded window. 'No, what we need at the moment is a dodgy accountant, to prepare figures for a bank-loan. Then we buy the equipment, sell it again as soon as we've done enough work to get the deposits rolling in, and fade quietly away. But where to find a bent accountant in a strange town, that I don't know.'

'If that's all you want . . . Remember that feller who pulled it together for us when we were doing swimming-pools?'

Harry blew smoke-rings while he thought back. 'Hancock?' he said at last.

'That's him. He's here.'

'I could use an hour or two of his time, if he's keeping off the hard stuff. Where's he staying?'

'He was just going into the Royal Hotel when I was on my way here.'

'Then he's probably too pissed to recognise us by now,' Harry said, standing up with an effort. 'But it's worth a try. Let's get round there before he ends up inside the bottle.'

In the cocktail bar of the Royal Hotel, Ted Hancock was getting quietly and inoffensively stoned. He knew that this was the beginning of the slide but he also knew that there was nothing he could do about it. His only concern was whether to claim sick-leave with the aid of a friendly doctor, in which case his salary would continue for some months, or to send in his resignation immediately in order to be eligible for good references in the future.

The half-remembered voice and the slap on his shoulder caught him off-guard and he needed a few seconds to orient himself. 'Mr Moyes?' he said at last.

'The same.'

Hancock lit up in a smile. He was one of the few who had had dealings with Harry Moyes and had emerged unscathed. 'While we're on the subject of liquidation, what'll you take?'

'I'll do it, Ted.' Harry beckoned to the barman, at the same time, behind Hancock's back, shaking his head to Walter Pratt. Hancock's eyes alone would have been enough to tell him that the man was drunk. Whether he would be of immediate use as a financial helper was doubtful, but a favour now might lead to a favour returned. Besides, like was calling to like.

The drinks arrived and they adjourned to a table in a quiet corner.

Ted sipped his new drink and then took a deep breath through his mouth, inhaling the fumes like a smoker taking a long draw. Experience had taught him that this was his best way to get the maximum mileage out of a given quantity. 'What line of business are you in now?' he asked. His voice was already beginning to slur.

'Tarmac,' Harry said. 'We can give you a good rate for your drive if you like,' he added. Friends may be friends, but business is business.

'Kind of you, but I don't have a drive. An', if I had, no way would I put cash up front. Don't want to hurt the feelings of an ol' pal, but cash on completion's the rule. When d'you plan to go bust?'

Harry shushed him quickly, glancing round at the other tables. 'We've only just set up here,' he said. 'These could be our customers.'

Ted laid a finger alongside his nose and winked. 'Sorry. 'Nuff said.'

'Judging from the signs, you'll be looking for some drinking-money soon,' Harry said. 'Bring us a few customers and we'll cut you in.'

Ted shook his head and then held on to the table until the room stopped swimming. 'Just passing through,' he said.

'Indeed?' The vagaries of Ted Hancock's journeyings were of no interest to Harry. 'Since we've met so fortuitously, you may care to give me some advice. I need a bank-loan.' He outlined the problem.

Hancock listened keenly, pondered and then pronounced. 'Forget about banks,' he said. 'Banks like to have other banks for referees. What you want's a "long firm" fraud. Do any of your old companies still exist?'

'Not as going concerns,' Harry said.

'All you need is other companies, still registered, with addresses and notepaper.'

Harry had to cast his mind a long way back. His more recent companies, those which had not been liquidated, might still be watched by creditors or by the Filbustini brothers. In most cases, the premises had long since been abandoned with the rent unpaid, but some had used accommodation addresses. 'I've got a few of those,' he said.

'Well then. Buy your machinery on tick. Give your other firms as references. Pick up the mail and write back, telling'm how solid and reliable a citizen you are.'

Walter was already nodding. Harry thought, and realised the sense in Ted's plan. 'You're right,' he said. 'We'll do it that way. It'll make a nice change. Keep in touch. If it works out, I'll send you a cut. What are you doing these days? Last I heard, you were with the National Bank.' The question was no more than a polite enquiry prior to breaking off a contact which had run its course.

'Still with 'em,' Ted Hancock said. 'In the City.'

'You're touring the branches?'

'Not branches. No.' Ted held his glass up to the light and found that it was empty. 'My turn,' he said.

'There's no need—' Harry began.

'Not to worry.' Ted took out a banknote. 'Next time I need money, I won't have to come to you for a commission. I know where I'll go.' He tried, without success, to rise.

'Walter can get them.' Harry pushed the note to his partner. Ted's words had intrigued him, but he knew better than to rush in. 'So you're on safari just now?' he suggested.

'Tha's right. Very important. In ... ter ... est ... ing.'

'Forgive my asking,' Harry said, 'but are you going to be able to stay with it? I seem to detect some faint signs of the backsliding to which I remember you were subject. It was your custom to tender your resignation.'

'This time, I just made up my mind I'll put in a sick-line and take the crash cure. Don't want to miss the end of this one.' Ted's hesitation was only momentary. He was too far gone to be discreet. 'Helping one of the bigwigs with an investigation. Matter of moment. 'Tween ourselves, somebody pulled off a fraud on the bank's main computer.'

Harry Moyes was now alert. His spiritual antennae, always searching for the smallest divergences in the ordered pattern of finance, were up and quivering. 'Inside job?' he asked as if by the way.

'Nah. We've ruled that out. Somebody hacked in their own computer from outside. We're doing the round of places it could've been done from.'

'I thought these institutional computers were protected with all sorts of codes and tricks,' Harry said. '"Encryption", they call it, don't they?'

'They are. By God they are! But the outsider can still get through. Usually happens first time by accident. There was a teenager in the States was playing with the family's computer and he came up on the mainframe at the Pentagon. His father said it was impossible. Can't you just see it? "You don't believe me, Dad? You want to see me fire a missile?" From what I hear, those members of the FBI who only got diarrhoea were the lucky ones. The rest had coronaries.'

'Seems to me,' Harry said slowly, 'you'll have time to

take the cure at your leisure. Your boss will be on tour for the rest of this year and most of next.'

'Not a bloody bit of it. One of the reasons this system was chosen was because there's not too many compatible mainframes. Less'n a dozen to go.' Walter came back with the fresh round of drinks. Ted took a quick sip and inhaled the delicious fumes. 'Tell you a funny thing. I already know who did it. Place we went to last week.'

'Does your boss know?'

'Not him. He's a clever sod around a computer, but he's a lazy bugger and randy with it, and outside of his own line he's as thick as dried horse-shit. He started off convinced the job was impossible, so everywhere we went he was too busy chasing a piece of tail to notice what was going on under his nose. But me, I keep my wits about me.' Ted winked solemnly. 'Eyes and ears open, mouth tight shut, that's my rules.'

Harry refrained from comment on this delusion. 'So what did your eyes and ears see and hear?' he asked.

'I saw two people who were nervous as hell. They talked too fast and too high.' In his excitement, Ted's own voice was rising. 'One of them was the bird he was chasing. I didn't even have to ask more than one or two questions, just to let people talk. And d'you know what I heard?'

'Tell me,' Harry said. 'But don't tell the whole bar. Keep your voice down.'

'I'm going to. I heard that this girl's a computer specialist with a sideline in security systems. Near as I can make out, about the time my boss was designing our software at Cambridge she was there as a post-graduate student. Usually, she uses a micro in the basement but about when it all happened she spent a lot of time on the University's mainframe computer. And –

67

get this – the University was talking redundancies because of shortage of funds. Now, the redundancy threat's been lifted. Hers was one of the jobs threatened.'

'Well I'll be . . .' Harry began. He stopped, unable to think of an epithet sufficiently extreme. 'You mean they switched funds into their employer's account?' To Harry Moyes, the concept smacked of perversion.

'That's not all. The girl,' Ted went on. 'The way she was described to me, she used to be two penn'orth of nothing, a mouse, dressed like the poor relation of somebody's poor relation, if you can imagine that. But between the time they'd've got our letter and the time we turned up, she got herself turned out like a royal's fancy-woman. Never looked at a man in her life, or so I'm told, but when the boss whistled she came running. And the next thing I know, we're moving on.'

'She had the pox or something?' Harry asked.

'Who knows? Whatever it was, she scared him shitless.'

'You do seem to have made good use of your natural talents,' Harry said. 'You haven't brought any of these most interesting facts to your boss's attention?'

Ted held his nose with one hand while he pulled an imaginary lavatory-chain with the other. 'Supercilious bugger,' he said. 'Treating this tour as a bloody good skive. 'Spects me to do the dirty work. Then he'd go back to Head Office an' give himself a nasty injury with patting himself on the back. Well, the hell with him.'

'What are you going to do?'

'Not decided. Could wait 'til we're back at the Head Office and he's put in a nil report to God and then drop'm in it by putting in a report of my own. More likely I'll stay dumb until I can go back and visit them for myself. Wouldn't cost them anything to switch some money my way. They've already got the key of the vault, see what I mean? There's enough there for everybody. How could they say no to me? One big tickle and away to the sunshine, where booze is cheap and girls do it because they want to.'

'I find your line of thought strangely intriguing,' Harry said. He took the unfinished drink out of Ted Hancock's hand. 'I think, Ted my boy, that you and I should have a little talk in the sober light of tomorrow, or, if that's too soon for you, the next day. Let me help you to your feet.'

EIGHT

Being on the run was not a new experience for Leo Gunn but it was unwelcome.

He had intended to phone somebody to tell them of Maud Venable's plight. But who, he asked himself wearily, could he have phoned? After his treatment of her, the fuzz would have had the story out of her in seconds.

By now, either she had been rescued or she had not. If rescued, she would know that he had left her to live or die by the luck of the draw and she would squawk like a rusty hinge. If she had not, then she was dead. Either way, he was in trouble.

Before leaving the flat, he had tried to eradicate all traces of his visits, polishing every surface which he could ever have touched. He had polished and left behind one of the pistols which he had taken off the Filbustinis – the other he had retained against his own possible need, but one was enough to conceal. He knew that it would only take one fingerprint, perhaps a ten-year-old latent, to set the hounds after him again. Maud was not the type to have kept a diary, but perhaps she had spoken incautiously to a friend. (It was Leo's belief that every girl-child was born with a certain number of words inside which she had to get out, in no particular order, before she could die in peace.' Or a neighbour might have described him. Or that bank-cashier, who had looked at him rather hard. Leo knew only too well how easy he was to describe.

There had been nothing in the papers or on the news. If she had been found dead, surely word would have leaked out. Were they playing it close to the chest? Or was her body still hanging there, silent and yet a ticking bomb? Leo remembered that he had always had a premonition that a woman would be the undoing of him, and he shivered whenever he thought about Maud.

He could do little to conceal his large size, except to cultivate a stoop and a mild manner which suggested a littler man, but he had learned to change his appearance in a hundred other ways and he used all of them. He moved like a fish beneath the surface of the ordered world, mingling with the sharks and the minnows alike, renewing old contacts.

He had to move with care. The Filbustinis would be watching for him. But although the brothers were seeking a foothold in the West End they had not yet obtained it in the teeth of longer-established and more powerful influences.

Leo was searching for somebody and he did not know who. His money was still in existence somewhere. If he knew how the system worked he could find out how to have a computer error remedied without attracting attention. Or, if he had been defrauded, he could find the culprits and then . . . Leo's huge hands twitched as he thought about how he would screw his money out of them. But first, he wanted an introduction to a man or woman who knew the world of banking, who would not talk and yet who could be trusted.

That was the rub. How to find somebody bent

enough to talk and straight enough to be trusted, and without asking the wrong person the wrong question?

Names were whispered to him, but not many. One, already known to him, belonged to a man who turned out to have quitted the country in some haste with the Fraud Squad on his tail. In an up-market coffee bar he met another, by appointment arranged through a bookmaker for whom Leo had once worked as an enforcer. He disliked the man's shifty eyes, fobbed him off with an improvised story and broke off contact with that whole section of his acquaintanceship.

That left only one name, which had been mentioned several times. 'You want Ted Hancock,' he was told by the proprietor of a small drinking-club. 'He may not be able to help if he's on the booze again, but at least he won't talk. Not talk as in grass.' Leo, who mistrusted drunks, was sceptical, but the other went on, 'Last I heard, he was on the wagon again and working for the National Bank.'

Leo phoned the bank from the call-box outside the club's Gents and was passed from extension to extension until, to his surprise, he reached the right department; but the voice, although friendly, was unhelpful. Mr Hancock was out of London indefinitely, travelling with Mr Boforth, the department head.

That in itself was good news. It suggested that Hancock was off the booze, and a different police area might provide a cooler working environment. But the voice refused, kindly but firmly, to reveal the whereabouts of the two men. Messages would be relayed or letters forwarded and that was all.

He needed another voice. For ten quid out of his remaining hoard, a tart with a voice like warm cream phoned the bank with an urgent personal message for Mr Boforth.

Quite by accident, he had hit on the right formula. The department secretary, who was still suffering from the after-effects of a brief romance with her boss, used the prerogative of a good secretary to make her own decision. If the caller was as pregnant as she sounded, it would be better if she were to overhaul her quarry in some distant corner of the country rather than to make a scene where God would be certain to hear about it.

One hour later, Leo was on a northbound train, swaying in the barcoach while he struggled to wash down a leaden sausage roll with weak lager.

At the Royal Hotel, he met with a setback. Hancock had already departed. The receptionist was chatty and she was turned on by big men. Mr Hancock, it seemed, had been taken ill and had left, leaving poor Mr Boforth absolutely in the lurch. A temporary replacement was due to arrive at any minute. No, Mr Hancock had left no forwarding address. If any mail arrived it was to be redirected to the bank.

Leo knew better than to take no for an answer. He kept his temper and, suppressing his aversion to the receptionist's blatant femininity, managed a little flirtation leavened with a touch of pathos. The receptionist remembered something else. She had seen Mr Hancock in the company of the two gentlemen who had the contract for resurfacing the hotel carpark. They might know where he had gone. And would the gentleman be staying?

The gentleman was not sure.

Leo walked the streets until he found the site where the portable building lurked among the weeds. Walter Pratt was standing by the battered desk, checking some paperwork, when Leo's large shadow fell across him.

On the wrong side of the law, most specialities are manned by loners but, in the vocation of fraud, paths tend to cross. It was a moment of mutual recognition.

'You, is it?' Leo said. 'So I don't suppose Harry Moyes is far away?'

'Not very,' Walter said cautiously. 'Nice to see you, Leo.'

'I just bet it is. You needn't try to crawl backwards through the wall, though by the state of the place that shouldn't be difficult. It's not you I'm after, nor Harry. Not this time. You know a banker called Hancock, Ted Hancock.'

Walter started to nod and then shook his head.

'Don't be a turd,' Leo said – quite gently, for him. He put out one hand and gripped Walter's shirt, taking with it a handful of muscle. He squeezed with steely fingers. Walter went up on his toes and whinnied. 'I don't have to rough you up,' Leo said. 'I been hearing things in the Smoke. I can always let the Filbustini brothers know where you are.'

'Let go my left tit,' Walter said shrilly. 'I'll tell you. I'll tell you. I'll tell you.'

Despite Leo's caution, it was inevitable that the Filbustinis would, sooner or later, cross his tracks. It was only by luck that the first scents which they had of him were already cold.

Although the brothers' main business was in property, they had more diverse interests. Property awaiting development can yield short-term profits. Like many another tycoon before them, the brothers found themselves promoted out of what they enjoyed and did well and were forced to spend more and more time on paperwork and on the supervision of those who now did the real work.

Some of their properties were suited to gambling, and these were let to a gaming syndicate in exchange for a share of the profits. Billy Ember's phone-call found the brothers in their flat, struggling with the accounts of the syndicate, quite sure that they had been ripped off but not sure for how much. The flat was luxuriously furnished with slightly dated modern furniture and two more blonde girls, one bleached and one for real.

Mark took the call. He listened for a few seconds, asked one question and then hung up. 'That was Billy,' he said. 'He wants us to meet him in a hurry where White Horse Lane leaves the Mile End Road. Something urgent.'

'Like what?'

'Nothing he was prepared to talk about on the phone.'

Pepe glowered. Little as he enjoyed his attempts to audit the syndicate's accounts, he hated to be called away. The effort of resuming would be all the greater. But Billy Ember, on the books as a rent-collector but in fact an eviction artist, was not one to summon help lightly. 'We'll have to go,' Pepe said reluctantly. 'Take the Merc?'

Mark looked down at the traffic hurrying past Kensington Gardens on the wet tarmac of Bayswater Road. 'Better by taxi, this time of day,' he said. 'There's damn-all parking around there. And that car's getting too well known. If Billy's got trouble, there's no point leading Mr Superintendent Bloody Eddlestone to it.'

Pepe nodded. Word had been passed that Superintendent Eddlestone was again taking an unhealthy interest in their comings and goings. He glanced at the two girls. 'Take messages. Say nothing.'

One of the girls nodded, without looking up from her magazine. Her job specification did not include idle chatter.

Taxis proved to be scarce and Billy Ember, waiting

on his corner, was almost hopping with anxiety when they arrived. He was a deceptively scrawny man, stronger than he looked and a tiger in a fight. 'You'd better come and see this for yourselves.' He led them round two corners and up some stairs to a flat over a butcher's shop. 'No rent this month, no answer at the door, so I let myself in. Here's what I found.'

The brothers walked through the prim, old-maidish flat. The heating had been off when Maud died and the north-facing living room was very cold. They looked at her dangling body without emotion. 'That the tenant?' Mark asked.

Billy nodded. 'That's her.'

'Get her out of here and we've got vacant possession. That makes almost the whole block, right?'

'Hold on,' Pepe said. 'Are you bloody blind?'

Mark looked around vaguely. The room was in good order. Not even a sign of condensation. The furniture . . . Suddenly, he saw it. On the cheap coffee-table, neatly placed in a central position and aligned with its long side, was an automatic pistol of familiar pattern. He pointed like a dog and homed in on it. 'Here!' he said.

'Don't touch it,' Pepe snapped. 'Not until we've thought it out.'

'But that's my bloody shooter. Look at the grips.'

His brother sighed in exasperation. 'Of course it's your bloody shooter,' he said. ' I saw that the moment we walked through the door. Think for a moment. How did it get here?'

Mark stood, blinking, for a moment before he remembered. 'Leo!' he said suddenly. 'He's been here.'

'Not a doubt of it. This is just Leo's scene. Hates women, but too scared of them to finish one off properly like a Christian.'

76

'Well, I'm not leaving it here,' Mark said. 'Those grips cost me money.'

Pepe clenched his fists and looked up at the ceiling. 'Christ! You're not thinking of keeping it? God knows who Leo mayn't've used it on before he dumped it here. Does she have any holes in her?' He nodded towards Maud.

'None that nature didn't intend,' Billy said. 'I looked before I even went to the phone.'

'You looked inside her mouth?' Pepe asked.

'Of course.'

Mark was a slower thinker than his brother but he usually caught up in the end. 'This was Leo's woman,' he said suddenly. 'They always said he had a bird somewhere. I bet she was keeping the money warm for him.'

'Maybe,' Pepe said. 'This could've been his way of stopping her talking. Or maybe she welshed on him. Think of that? Either way, the money's still around.'

'Are you sure?'

'Sure as I can be. I keep getting whispers about Leo still being in town and trying to make contact with a money-man. The way I see it, that could mean he's still looking for help getting it out of the country. You realise what this means? It means that if we can catch up with Leo, we've got him. Really got him!'

Mark nodded slowly. 'What do we do?' he asked.

'Let's think.' While he thought, Pepe regarded Maud with a dispassionate stare. 'You take your shooter away,' he said at last, 'and lose it. Keep the grips, if you must, to put on another one, but that one's got to go. We touch nothing else, absolutely nothing. "Preserving the scene" they call it. This is Leo's crime and nobody else's and we may want the law to be able to prove it.'

'Will she last that long?' Mark asked.

Pepe removed a glove and prodded the dead buttock with his finger. 'She'll last,' he said. 'It's cold and dry in here. She got something off the rent because of the cold. It's over the cold store downstairs and the insulation's buggered. She's starting to mummify. Come on outside.' But he stopped in the tiny hall, so suddenly that the others bumped into him. 'The last thing we want's for some yobbo to break in. Once the fuzz find her, our leverage with Leo's gone.'

'We could board up the door,' Billy suggested.

'Not boards,' Pepe said. 'Boards are an invitation, not a deterrent. Anybody can pull them off again. What we want is . . .something which looks as if it's always been there. We want the door reinforced with a steel plate and a couple of better locks.'

'I'll get somebody on to it,' Billy said.

'You'll get nobody on to it.' Pepe raised both fists and shook them. 'Am I surrounded by idiots? How can you bring some workman into the place and trust him not to wonder why there's a rope over that door? I'll get back to those accounts. You two buy the stuff and do the job. Get the plate cut and drilled before you carry it in. Paint it to match. Don't leave any prints and, when you've finished, wipe the keys off and leave them in her handbag. Got it?'

'Got it,' the others said together.

'You'd bloody better. When we've got what we want out of Leo you can come back and take her away.'

'Then what do we do with her?' Mark asked.

'What do I care? By that time she'll probably make a good standard lamp. That was a joke,' Pepe added quickly. Sometimes his brother took him too literally.

NINE

Polly Holt was the most junior member of staff to be
elected to the Staff Club. Her election was an honour
but she made only occasional use of the premises. In
them, she felt humbled by the sheer weight of assembled brains.

Although after three weeks she had allowed her new
standard of grooming to slip a little, this only allowed
formal elegance to be replaced by casual charm. As she
moved through the Coffee Room, she was still both
feminine and alluring and she walked with a newly
acquired arrogance. She felt surreptitious male eyes on
her like hot hands as she carried her coffee through the
lounge. The sensation was not as displeasing as she had
once expected.

She found her quarry finishing his lunch. Dr Westerly
rose as she approached. He would not have thought of
such a courtesy a month ago.

'Would you meet me in the Computer Room as soon
as you can?' Polly asked.

'I suppose so. But I've an appointment in a few
minutes. What—?'

'Confidential and very urgent,' she broke in. A
garrulous professor was sharing Dr Westerly's table.

Westerly felt anxiety clutch at his vitals. 'I'll come now.' Still standing he drained his coffee-cup and followed Polly out of the room. They shared the lift with two secretaries, so they travelled in silence.

They found Dr Helinger taking his own coffee in the Computer Room.

'I think we've got something to worry about,' Polly said as soon as she was inside the door. 'Somebody's been through my room.'

Peter Helinger sat up with a jerk and nearly spilled his cup. 'I don't see how you could tell,' he said. 'Your room always looks as if it's been searched.'

'It's a shambles, but an orderly shambles,' Polly said. 'I can only live with it that way because I know exactly where everything is. My system may not be much of a system, but such as it is it works for me. And suddenly, this morning, everything's different. I keep putting my hand out to pick something up from where I know it is, and it's somewhere else.'

'The cleaners?' Dr Westerly suggested. 'For God's sake sit down,' he added. 'You're making us dizzy.'

Polly, who had been pacing the room, dropped into a chair. 'The cleaners sweep the floor and that's all. I've threatened them with all sorts of doom if they lay a finger on anything else.'

Westerly looked at her white face and moist eyes. 'Calm down,' he said. 'If there's nothing there, a search can't do any harm.'

'But it means that somebody suspects,' she said. 'And suspects me. Maybe we weren't convincing enough. Damn it, it's all very well for you. You talked us into this and now you sit back telling me to calm down. Nobody suspects you. You didn't do anything. And I'm the one who . . . who . . .'

'Accepting all that,' Westerly said, '– and I'm sorry

you feel that way about it – I go back to what I said at the beginning. Listen to me carefully, because I'm talking sense.' He emphasised his points with a raised finger. 'Sit tight, say nothing and do even less and nobody can prove anything against any of us, not unless you now give him something fresh to work on by acting out-of-key. At the very worst, Boforth may have the feeling that he could have been out-manoeuvred and has sent somebody back to re-check.'

'God, I hope you're right,' Helinger said.

'So do I,' Polly said. 'But one of the janitors told me that he found somebody in the room and turned him out because students shouldn't be alone in private rooms. He said that he was very young, with a smile like a cupboard full of white china. That doesn't sound like anybody from the bank.'

For some seconds they were trapped in a bubble of silence.

'It doesn't sound like anybody from the police either,' Westerly said at last. 'Probably a coincidence, or a spot of industrial espionage.'

'Nobody would do industrial espionage in my room,' Polly protested.

'You don't know that. Your various systems for preventing the copying of videos are widely used. There's a lot of money in video piracy these days.'

'Maybe he really was a student,' Helinger said. 'We could get the janitor to point him out, just to set our minds at rest.'

'No, no, a thousand times no,' said Westerly. 'That's just the kind of action which might confirm somebody's suspicions. Haven't I got through to you at all?' Westerly looked at his watch. 'I wish I had time to stand guard over you, but now I must love you and leave you. I'm already late for an appointment with an army

81

major. He seems to be under the impression that a talk from me about international economics might help his squaddies to manage their pay-packets better. And – who knows? – he may even be right.

'Meantime,' Westerly added, 'the order of the day is a masterly inactivity. I have been specialising in that for years, so watch me and learn.'

'I should do what the doctor suggests,' said a cheerful voice from the door. Three heads jerked round. A man in his thirties, immaculate in a well-cut suit and carrying gloves, hat and a tightly rolled umbrella, was smiling absently at them. 'Those are the kind of orders I've been hoping for for years. Sorry if I made you jump.'

'This is Major Craythorne,' Dr Westerly said shakily. 'It's for me to apologise, Major. I'm late for our appointment.'

'More masterly inactivity, perhaps? You don't evade me so easily. Your department suggested that I might find you over here. They were going to phone for you, but I said that I'd walk across. Computers seem to be figuring ever larger, even in my low-tech sphere, so I'd be interested in seeing the place, assuming that there are no deep secrets lying around. Won't you introduce me?'

'This is Miss Holt,' Westerly mumbled. 'And Dr Helinger.' His colleagues managed no more than a nod and a shaky smile apiece.

'Delighted,' said Craythorne, 'but, actually, I meant introduce me to the computer.'

When Steven Moyes was a child, in the not so very distant past, he was quite unable to pronounce his own name. The nearest approach that he could make to it was 'Teeth', so as Teeth he was, more or less affectionately, known. Only when his baby-teeth were replaced by a set which, so his family averred with more humour than originality, needed only the appropriate inscriptions to be mistaken for white marble tombstones was the aptness of the nickname recognised.

For several years, while he passed slowly through adolescence, the soubriquet was stretched to 'Teeth-and-spots', a description so exact that the post office managed to deliver correctly a valentine so addressed by a young lady who was uncertain as to his real name and house-number.

The acne had passed, leaving only a slightly macho pitting of his complexion, and Teeth he remained. He was a flashily good-looking boy, except that new acquaintances were liable to assume that he was wearing an inexpensive set of dentures. Girls, once they had come to accept his overpowering smile, seldom resisted him for long. He seemed hardly to be into long trousers before his reluctantly admiring father was paying out for the first affiliation order against him.

At school, Teeth had not otherwise shone. Until his final year, only the school dentist among the staff had pointed him out with pride. His school reports had been couched in terms such as 'lacks both application and aptitude' and were unanimous in suggesting that some lowly, manual occupation requiring minimal skills might suit him best.

Then, at the last minute, one subject had redeemed his scholastic record. Elementary arithmetic had been beyond him but, to Teeth, the advanced levels of the New Maths made more sense than they had to his reluctantly converted teachers. When, as an experiment, he was introduced to the school's computers, it was found that he was one of the precious new breed who had a natural affinity with them. He would have taken them for walks if he could.

It was, therefore, only natural that his Uncle Harry

Moyes should think of him and that Teeth, who had just completed an MSC course in Information Technology and was conducting a research programme to discover how long he could postpone the search for a job, hurried to his uncle's side.

Harry had had no difficulty persuading Ted Hancock to claim sick-leave and go with them. As always when on the down-slide away from reality, Hancock was easily led and his moral senses were out of focus.

When Leo Gunn, unannounced, walked into Harry's room in the Oaken Tree, the three – if Ted could still be counted as a whole person – had been on the job for a little more than forty-eight frustrating hours and were holding a gloomy conference.

Leo looked around the room with distaste. The Oaken Tree is an old-fashioned hotel with large and gracious rooms, but Harry and his companions failed to live up to it. All three had drinks, but Ted was wrapped lovingly around the bottle. Cigar and cigarette stubs filled the ashtray and the room was thick with smoke. Leo crossed the room in three strides and threw open the window. Traffic noise rushed in and the fresh air struck at them.

'Who the hell are you?' Teeth demanded.

Harry moved with unwonted speed. One did not speak to Leo in such terms if one had any aspirations to old age. Leo lifted his fist, but Harry was already out of his chair and between them. 'Leave it to me. Please, Leo. This is Leo Gunn,' he told Teeth. 'Be polite. Remember all your mother told you and a little more.' Seeing Leo's big fist unclench, Harry relaxed a little. 'Hullo, Leo, You're back in circulation, then?'

'You can see I am. Who or what is this?'

'My nephew,' Harry said apologetically. 'He's known as Teeth.'

'He'd have to be. So this must be Ted Hancock?'

Ted smiled uncertainly. Even allowing for the exaggerated size, which he put down to the onset of his hallucinations, Leo was not a comforting sight.

'That's right,' Harry said. 'What can we do for you, Leo?'

'You, nothing. I've come a long way to have a word with Hancock, but maybe I've wasted my trip.'

'You want us to leave you two alone?' Harry asked eagerly. It was never safe to relax fully when Leo was around.

'Don't bother,' Leo said after a moment's thought. 'Sit down. The bugger looks incoherent. Maybe you can interpret for me. You speak alcoholic? And if you're not afraid enough of me to keep your mouth shut—'

'I am, Leo. I am.'

'—just remember that I can let the Filbustini brothers know where you are.'

Harry looked wounded. 'There's no need for that sort of talk, Leo. You know I can keep my mouth shut.'

'I knew you could. Now I know you will.' Leo seated himself on the bed and reached out to take the bottle out of Ted's limp hand. 'Can you hear me?' he asked.

'I hear you.' Ted's eyes opened and then began to close again.

'Listen good. I got a current account with the National Bank. A hundred and fifty grand went missing out of it. You tell me how that could happen. Could it be computer error? Or could the law have put a stopper on it?'

Ted's eyes shot open and came into focus. 'Stepney Branch?' he asked.

'You know about it?'

Harry Moyes tried to give Ted a warning look but failed to make eye-contact. He sat back. It was already too late . . . and Leo's participation might even turn out to be a boon.

Ted tried to sit up but his hand slid off the arm of his chair and he nearly fell over. He settled himself safely. 'Wasn't the law,' he said thickly. 'You the depositor? Careful, but not careful enough. Set the bank-staff wondering. That's why I been scampering round country last weeks, looking where leak went.'

His verbal shorthand was understood. Leo considered for a few seconds. 'Not an inside job, then?'

Ted had passed the point at which he could still shake his head. 'Definitely not,' he said. 'Couple academics local college.'

'You know who it was?' Leo got to his feet in a sudden fever. 'Come and point them out to me.' He started to pull Ted Hancock to his feet but the accountant's legs had turned to rubber and Leo found himself supporting a limp body by its lapels.

'Just one holy minute,' Harry said desperately. 'Leo, what do you think you're going to do?'

'I'll . . . I'll do something,' Leo said. 'Don't know what yet. Kill them, probably. Nobody gets away with my money, by God!'

'You'll bugger up the best thing since King Midas.'

Leo frowned awfully and seemed to swell until the walls of the room were forced to retreat. 'I don't know what you got going,' he said, 'and I don't care. You stay out of my way or I'll flatten you. I want my hundred and a half back.'

'Yours particularly?'

'Course it is.'

'You don't understand me,' Harry said. 'What I mean is, are you set on having that money in particular back, or would any old hundred and fifty grand do?'

Leo tossed Ted into his chair and sat back on to the

bed. 'What d'you mean?'

'Your hundred and fifty K is gone where you'll never get it back, not without alerting the fuzz. Right, Ted?'

'No shadow doubt.'

'But this pair,' Harry resumed, 'they've cracked it. They know how to bypass the bank's security codes and if you can do that you can write your own cheques on any account in the bank. We were going after the pair of them, to find out what they know. Then we'll settle for a million or two apiece and be over the horizon long before anyone knows it's gone. You want a piece of that, join in with us. There's plenty for everybody.'

Leo thought it over. It sounded good. Only one thing stuck in his gullet. 'And let them keep my money?'

'It isn't your money now,' Harry said patiently. He was feeling more confident. 'It never really belonged to you any more than it now belongs to whoever's got it. If we're talking about the money you went inside for, my guess is that it still belongs to the underwriters. Anyway, they don't have it any more.'

Leo blinked at him. He had been thinking of the money as his for far too long to accept the idea of any other ownership. He prodded Ted in the chest. 'What did they do?' he demanded.

Ted held out his empty glass and Leo dribbled a little whisky into it. Ted sipped. 'Best guess,' he said, 'connected computer by chance. Thought it was Christmas. Dunno how they broke codes – I work that department, couldn' do it myself. Must've done random hunt current accounts for big one wi' no transactions.'

Leo, listening intently, grunted. Hong Kong might have been a mistake after all. 'And then?' he asked.

'Bank's total balances OK, far as tell – always cash in transit. So transfers were to accounts with bank.

Withdrawls could come later. Then close any inter . . . intermeddary accounts and tell computer forget all about it. Couldn' be simpler.'

'And we could do the same?'

'Easy as wink. If we get codes. And phone-number.'

Leo scowled. 'Don't try to fart around,' he said. 'You can get the phone-number.'

Ted waved a hand in a vague but recognisably negative gesture. 'Can't ask Directory Enquiries. Nobody, but nobody, allowed it. All done by Autodiallers, an' they're locked up tighter than the money every night. Secret guarded closely as princess's virginity. No, closer'n that. Much.'

Ted seemed to doze off. Leo brooded and then looked at Harry. 'How far have you got?'

Harry nodded towards Teeth, who bared his fangs in a shy smile. 'I brought my nephew in,' Harry said, 'because he cut those teeth on computers. He did the recce because he'd have the best chance of spotting what we want, and because he's young enough to pass for a student. Tell him, Teeth.'

'Go on, then, Gnashers,' Leo said. 'Tell us all about it.'

Teeth cleared his throat nervously. 'I wandered around all day yesterday and some of this morning. Nobody seemed to give much of a damn. Lots of departments have microcomputers, but Ted says it couldn't have been done from one of them. There's an old mainframe in the Computer Department—'

'That's where it was done from?'

'Likely enough. There's several terminals to it in other departments, but they mostly belong to small science departments using it in an unsophisticated way as a sort of big boys' calculator. I reckon Ted's right. The computer boss and the girl. The bird would have done the magic bit. I went through her room while she was out – invigilating, whatever that means. It's full of stacks and stacks of paper and tapes. The papers all seemed to be what it said on the boxes, mostly to do with security codes. Nothing seemed to be deliberately hidden, but without running every tape and disc through the computer there's no way of telling what she's got tucked away on them and labelled as something else. She has a micro in her room, and I'm told she has another of her own at home.'

'You didn't leave any signs of a search?' Leo asked sharply.

'Don't think so. The place is like a pig-sty, so it wasn't easy to replace things as they were. But the janitor turfed me out yesterday, and this morning the Computer Room chief walked in on me and turfed me out again. The janny was only being officious, but I think the other man suspected something.'

'I doubt if it matters much,' Harry put in before Leo could erupt. 'It might be to the good to keep them worried. The last thing we want is for them to sit tight. I did wonder about tipping them off – "Fly at once, all is discovered", that sort of thing. We could have watched to see who panicked and what they tried to hide.'

'Nah,' Leo said. 'Too chancy. Either of them have relatives?'

'They both live alone,' Teeth said.

Harry preferred deviousness to violence. 'For God's sake, Leo,' he said, 'let's not think about kidnapping. Not yet, anyway. It needs planning and preparation, and then you've got the problem of whether the victims can put the finger on you afterwards. Let's go on as we are and try to find the data first.'

'You're sure they haven't already destroyed all of that? You. Joe Soak.' Leo gave Ted an ungentle kick.

Ted opened his eyes. 'Definitely,' he said. 'Couldn't remember it all. And never was an academic yet who'd throw away piece of original research. 'S against their religion.'

'Then,' Leo said decisively, 'the first thing's to see if we can get our hands on those papers or whatever.'

'That's what I just said,' Harry pointed out.

Leo ignored him. 'You, Gnashers. That's your job.'

'I already tried,' Teeth said plaintively.

'Try harder and again. You tried her office. You really think she'd keep evidence of a crime at her work, where some technician could come across it? Try her home.'

'Me? I've never done no burglary!'

'Never too early to start learning a trade,' Leo said, unsmiling. 'Your uncle's not going to start at his time of life and I'm too big to get through windows. And, as he says, you're the one who knows what to look for.'

'It's down to you, Teeth,' Harry said. 'You're in a new ballgame now. Stiffen the sinews, summon up the blood.'

'Don't mention blood,' Teeth said. 'I wouldn't know how to begin breaking and entering.'

'I'll bloody tell you how to begin,' Leo said. 'Dress up respectable, but with shoes you can run in, just in case. You're going to knock on the door, so have a good story ready in case somebody answers it. You can take a good look from a distance first, to see which windows aren't overlooked. You want a few simple tools—'

'The shops are shut,' Teeth said desperately.

'They'll open in the morning.'

'We don't even know where she lives.'

Leo's patience gave out. 'Look in the bloody phone-book,' he roared.

TEN

Mark Filbustini was waiting, as usual, for his brother. Pepe was at the other end of the bar, buying information from a casino employee. The basement drinking-club was a dingy hole, its only merit being its exemption from the hours of opening decreed under the licensing laws.

Mark was profoundly dissatisfied with life. True, he and his brother were making money. Such of their property as was not yet ripe for development was mostly occupied, willingly or unwillingly, by girls with real looks and class or, if too slummy for the girly trade, over-occupied by cowed immigrants. Their few really high-class houses were shared with the casino operators. All in all, it was a lucrative business. But what did the money bring, he asked himself yet again. Booze and girls, but he had never been short of either. And leisure which, for him, was synonymous with boredom. He did not have the mental resources to cope with idleness.

The plushy life was all very well, but he yearned sometimes for the good old days, when they had been making their mark at the expense of the opposition. That was when he had been a real man. Others might daydream of sex or luxury or of idleness in the

Caribbean, but Mark Filbustini lacked the imagination for fantasising. When he daydreamed it was to re-create in his mind the remembered pleasure of seeing the confidence in a hard man's eyes replaced by uncertainty, followed by fear and then stark terror. Perhaps it was time to put the rents up again, just for the sake of the aggro.

Mark fetched another drink and tried to count his blessings.

His brother was in a foul mood these days. Well, they had been taken twice that year. Mark, although never one to look for the silver lining, was less inclined to take the two failures personally. Neither caper, after all, would have taken money out of their pockets if Pepe, in a fit of temper, hadn't been fool enough to refuse Harry Moyes' offer to return their deposit. As a compensation, some day they might catch up with Harry or, even better, with Leo Gunn. Again, Mark had not particularly minded waiting in the rain for a new set of clothes. It had been almost worth it for the pleasure of seeing the stuck-up Honourable Brenda slinking off, bare-arsed, to find an unlit phone-box, with Pepe's red handprint still etched on her backside. Perhaps when they met Leo again, Pepe's restraining influence would not be so evident . . .

At this thought, his habitually ferocious expression softened for a moment, so that a late-teenager in black leather, whose courage had almost failed him, dared to approach.

Mark looked at the newcomer without interest. 'What the hell do you want, Piddling?'

Clem Pilling swallowed audibly but nerved himself to sit down, the better to communicate softly. ''Eard you was looking for somebody.'

Mark brightened. 'Leo Gunn?'

'Who? The word I got was that you wanted to know about Harry Moyes.'

Mark shrugged. Second-best would do. 'You know where he is?'

'Not for sure. But Steven Moyes – Teeth – got a letter from him. There was money in it. And now Teeth's gone out of town. I'd guess he's gone to join his uncle.'

'You know where?'

'Only the town. Went to the station with him when he bought his ticket, didn't I?'

Mark Filbustini thought it over, slowly but surely. He was not inclined to dash around the country on such slim evidence, and the sight of his unmistakable figure would be enough to send his quarry running. He took two large notes out of a fat wallet and laid them on the table. 'Get out there,' he said. 'Don't frighten him. Unless you fancy carving him up for me?' he added maliciously.

Clem Pilling shivered, half-pleasurably. 'Not me,' he said.

'Thought not. Well, if you can spot Harry Fuckin' Moyes, phone me. There'll be fifty more for you.'

They parted. Each was in a more cheerful frame of mind. Clem was looking forward to the money and to having the friendship and protection of the Filbustini brothers. Mark was looking forward to doing something very nasty to Harry Moyes, his pleasure enhanced by knowing that the retribution to come was deserved. Nobody, but nobody, must get away with conning the Filbustinis. It only takes one pebble to start a landslide.

That same evening, a message reached them from Clem Pilling. He had spotted Harry Moyes in the act of collecting a car from a car-hire firm but, not yet being a driver, had lost him again for the moment.

The brothers conferred. Pepe now had a good idea

where in the casino operation the money was being diverted. He intended to get proof by sending a quartet of hirelings to count the take for an evening while trying not to lose too much at the tables.

'I'd better stick around, then,' Mark said. 'They won't cough up without a fight.'

'There'll be no fighting,' Pepe said. 'One of Eddlestone's coppers followed me around all afternoon. If the syndicate won't cough up what they've short-changed us, plus interest and compensation, that's the end of their leases. They'll cough up before that happens. Diplomacy, that's what we want around here, not violence. You can be as rough as you like up north.'

Mark went north alone the following morning, by train. It was better that the distinctive Mercedes was not seen where the action was going to be. He deposited his pigskin suitcase at the nearest hotel and followed the hall porter's directions to the car-hire firm.

Clem Pilling was in a café across the road, drooping biliously over his eleventh fizzy drink of the day. He had already established, by chatting up the frizzy-haired bird behind the desk at the car-hire firm, that Harry Moyes had expected to return the hire-car to the same depot that day.

Mark hired another car and they settled down to wait in it. They were uncomfortable, but less so than in the café. When the street was empty Mark, who was in benign mood, showed Clem how to dismantle the Walther which now carried his personalised grips.

Its predecessor had been consigned to Father Thames under the watchful eye of Pepe. Mark, while he could see the reasoning, resented the waste. Unregistered, black-market pistols did not come free with a tankful of petrol.

* * *

94

Superintendent Ewan Eddlestone was an elderly man with a long nose and baggy eyes. His resemblance to a bloodhound, appropriate as it was, did not stop at the physical. He had reached his rank because he could follow a trail long after others believed it to be cold.

The Filbustinis' would be the last trail which he would follow and it appeared to be hopeless. Retirement, unwelcome but compulsory, was above the horizon and seemed to be approaching faster with every passing day. His hatred of the brothers was no sudden explosion of wrath but had grown slowly over several years, nurtured by whisper after whisper about violence, prostitution, Rachmanism, drugs and pornography.

So far, the brothers had emerged from their various brushes with the law almost unscathed. Their minions had been sent down for everything up to murder, but each took his medicine in silence. This universal loyalty to the brothers was not the outcome of love or in the hope of generous treatment on release; fear was the deterrent and they used it with skill and enthusiasm.

Superintendent Eddlestone knew this, just as he knew that jurors and even policemen had been threatened or bribed in order that the Filbustinis should remain in business. But knowing is not proving. Eddlestone's personal file on the Filbustinis was as detailed as the official records and considerably more interesting. If he could put the Filbustinis away, he would retire happy, his duty done, content with his roses and his memories.

At the moment, the prospect of such an outcome did not look good. Frankly, he thought that he had a better chance of becoming Pope, staunch Methodist though he was, but he knew better than to say so. Once a subordinate knew that success was not expected, any chance of success was gone. He looked round the table at the assembled officers – one chief inspector, three inspectors and a nervous sergeant – and he forced a confident smile as he recapitulated the sad facts.

'We know a great deal about the Filbustinis,' he said. 'We know, without a shadow of doubt, that they're behind half the crime on our patch. We know more than enough to send them away for ever . . . if we could only prove it. For proof we need witnesses. You have your informants. But not one of them is prepared to testify in court.'

'That's the way it is,' said one of the inspectors. 'Too many potential witnesses in the past have been carved up or just plain vanished. They don't believe promises of protection any more. They know that the protection we can give them's only a token.'

'And short-term,' the superintendent said gloomily. 'One of these days we'll maybe get a witness who doesn't have any relatives and doesn't mind going abroad. But I don't fancy holding my breath until that happens. What else haven't we tried?'

'In the old days,' the chief inspector said, 'we'd have fitted them up.' It was a carefully disguised suggestion.

'Those days are long gone,' Eddlestone said. He had given serious consideration to the possibility but had decided that nothing short of the truth would sink the Filbustinis. Otherwise, the brothers would match every lying witness with three of their own.

'They always come a cropper in the end, men like that,' said the same inspector. He was chasing promotion and felt that he had to make a show. Even if old Eddlestone was on the brink of retirement, he might leave a complimentary note on file. 'Usually it's one of their own men that cracks. Are we giving enough attention to their associates?'

'We have done,' Eddlestone said. 'They're usually the

most scared of all, because they know better than anyone else what the Filbustinis are capable of. But maybe you're right, we've been letting up on the lower ranks. It's time we put the word round all the divisions again, to let me know the minute one of the Filbustini gang gets nicked for anything. Anything at all.'

The sergeant was only present to make notes and run errands, but he was interested. 'Excuse me, sir,' he said, 'but do we have a list of all the Filbustinis' men?'

Eddlestone looked sharply at him but remembered that it would be the sergeant's job to pass the word along. 'Here you are,' he said, passing over a paper from his file. 'These are all I know about. CRO might have a few more. I want to be told if one of those men so much as spits on the pavement.'

The sergeant ran his eye down the list. 'Here!' he said. 'It says Billy Ember. There was a W. Ember taken up yesterday for disorderly conduct. Other charges pending, including GBH. Could it be the same man?'

'Don't sit there asking stupid questions,' Eddlestone said. 'Bloody well go and find out, quick.'

Polly Holt rented what had once been a pair of farmworkers' cottages, set in land which had not yet been transformed into a replica of the American prairie but remained an attractive patchwork of fields separated by hedges to shelter both crops and wildlife.

But she seldom noticed the view or the rich ecology which surrounded her. The cottages had been built for families with low aspirations and in no position to complain, so that the rooms were dark, impossible to heat and tended to dampness, but that hardly mattered. The conversion had been made with taste, using coloured renders and bright paintwork, but that was of equal unimportance. What mattered was that there was a shed for her beloved Mini and plenty of space for her personal computer and large collection of books. That there was also room to eat, sleep and bath was a bonus. She had settled cheerfully into a carefully organised muddle.

To Leo and Harry, and to a lesser extent to Teeth, the place seemed ideal from a criterion quite other than that of the occupant. Harry brought the hired car to a halt where they could see through a gap in a tall hedge and across a field occupied by what he thought were probably cows to where the cottage sat, bland in the sunshine, beside a farm-road and backed by a tall wood. 'Perfect,' he said. 'Not overlooked at all.'

'Sash and case windows,' Leo said. 'No need to break glass. You only got to slip a blade up the crack.'

'No alarm on the outside,' said Harry. 'And no sign of life. She's away at work. You'll be getting spoiled. Off you go.'

'She could still be there,' Teeth said. 'Garage doors are shut. The exams are almost over.'

'Well, you got your story,' Leo said impatiently. 'Get on with it.'

Teeth sighed as loudly as he could and got out of the car. As he plodded round three sides of a square – nothing would have lured him into that field – he told himself that he had come along as a consultant, not as a creeper. In his dudgeon, he added another nought to the figure which he had decided to embezzle for himself.

Off the farm-road, a few yards of track had been upgraded by a dozen loads of gravel into what could be called a drive. Approaching the door, Teeth glimpsed a fuel-oil tank lurking among some overgrown shrubs. He put a final polish on his story. The offer of regular deliveries of Coke should prove suitably unacceptable. He pressed the bell-push. The season and the time for birdsong were both past. The house and garden were in silence, a silence such as Teeth had never known before in his citybound years, and he felt an unease in his sphincter.

He was about to slip the table-knife out of his sleeve when he realised that he had not heard the sound of the bell. He rattled the flap of the letterbox and waited again. The sun was warm on his back and he could feel the eyes of Leo and his uncle.

Polly Holt, silent in slippers, reached the door. The door groaned as it opened, covering a sound from Teeth's nervous bowel. She looked at him, stiff with suspicion. If he had smiled, she might have been struck by his resemblance to the janitor's description – 'Very young, with a mouth like a cupboard full of white china.' But Teeth felt very unlike smiling. He looked so terrified that after a moment she relaxed.

'You're one of the students, aren't you?' she said. 'I've seen you around.'

Teeth had been on the point of producing a story which he could now see would have been disastrous. He threw away the script. 'Sorry to bother you at home,' he mumbled, 'but you weren't in the department this morning. I got a computing problem. Thought you might help. But if I'm being a nuisance I'll bugger off. Begging your pardon.'

'Oh?' She hesitated. It was a long way for a student to come, but most of them had motorbikes or old bangers. Some had cars which were worth her salary over several years. 'It must be urgent, to bring you all this way.'

'It is, a bit,' Teeth said. 'But, even if it hadn't been, I'd've come anyway. There's something I couldn't say around the University. I think you're the nicest-looking bird I've ever seen.'

There was some justification in the compliment.

Polly might not always maintain the high standard set her by Patricia Helinger, but that morning, after correcting terminal exam-papers far into the night, she had slept late, only finishing her after-breakfast shower shortly before Teeth's arrival. Her hair, tinted to bring out its faintly auburn shade, fell readily into the new style which had been designed to enhance its natural wave and the shape of her face. Flushed from her shower and smelling faintly of perfumed soap, she had little need for makeup. In a rose-pink, quilted dressing-gown – the only spontaneous purchase which she had ever made that suited her – she had, instead of beauty, the sort of ingénue, girl-next-door charm which film producers search for, usually in vain.

Teeth had known girls before, some of them pretty or even beautiful, but any of them would have looked cheap by comparison. This was his first exposure to a girl with brains, education and . . . class. That was the word.

Teeth had been appalled to hear the words spring from his mouth and he waited for the wrath which never came. Since her transmogrification and her surprising enchantment of Vernon Boforth, there had from time to time, among the ebb and flow of formulae and binary digits which usually occupied her mind, obtruded the thought that there might after all be something in this mating game. She had even wondered whether she did not have a special Power to Attract Men. The thought had been enough to make her wriggle in her lonely bed. And now, here was this moderately attractive boy . . .

'You'd better come in and have a coffee,' she said. 'Then we'll see what we can do. But I don't think that you should refer to members of staff as birds.'

'Girl, then,' Teeth said bravely. 'I think you're the

nicest-looking girl I've ever seen. Is that better?'

'Much better,' Polly said.

It was more like a man's home than a woman's, Teeth thought, except that it was scrupulously clean. It took him a few minutes to realise that the contents were not arranged for visual effect but so as to be at hand where they would be wanted next. By that time, Polly, still in her dressing-gown, had made coffee and dumped her breakfast dishes in the sink and they were sitting at the kitchen table. 'So what's the problem?' she asked.

Teeth had had time to refine his new story. 'I got my own micro at home,' he said. 'I do some work for a mate of mine. He's a bookie and he's got his own way of making sure the odds are right. We've got the record of every horse on disc now, with the length of race and type of going, and the program we wrote together comes closer to the right odds than I'd have believed. Makes a lot of money for my pal, the system. Trouble is, I think my stepbrother's using it when I'm out. He's taken some money off my pal, and my pal's not pleased.'

'So lock up your discs,' Polly said.

'Tried that,' Teeth said. He thought frantically and found the answer waiting, 'We think he's already copied the records. My mate had the disc with the program away with him at the time, so he didn't get to copy that. See, I know when he was buying discs. But we can't be sure of keeping it out of my stepbrother's reach for ever. If we could just make it uncopyable and also give it a security code . . .'

'Interesting,' Polly said. 'What make of micro and what language.'

Heads together and each very conscious of the other's presence, they explored the world of electronic coding systems, balancing confidentiality against convenience.

Teeth found that he could keep up his end of the technical discussion.

Several times, Polly left the kitchen to consult a file in another room. The first time, she delayed just long enough to apply a little makeup and to run a comb through her hair. She decided not to waste time in getting dressed.

Peter Helinger was standing in the quadrangle, absently admiring a climbing hydrangea in blue flower while thinking about multiple disc-drives, when he was joined by Hector Westerly.

'No more complications?' Westerly asked anxiously.

Dr Helinger remembered that he had more to worry about than the technical details of equipment still to be ordered. 'I don't honestly know,' he said slowly. 'I walked into Polly's room yesterday. There was a studentish type nosing around. A shifty-looking youngster with a flashing set of choppers.'

They fell silent as a group of students hurried past.

'Did he have dirty blond hair?' Westerly asked when the students were out of earshot.

'As far as I remember.'

'That boy, or somebody damn like him, was nosing round the Accountancy terminal the day before yesterday. He could be one of Boforth's minions.' Dr Westerly stared up at the sky. He looked so anxious that a passing lecturer followed his glance, expecting rainclouds. 'What's more, he sounds very like the boy who, according to Polly and one of the janitors, was snooping in her room.' He paused again. 'I think we'd better go and have a word with young Polly,' he said at last.

'She's having a day off, with my blessing.'

'Do you have her number? I'd be happier if we reminded her that we're whiter than white as long as we do and say absolutely nothing. Provided, of course, that she's destroyed all her notes as she promised. Do you suppose that she did so?'

'I'd be amazed if she had,' Helinger said. 'She's one of nature's prize hoarders of obsolete information.'

'I wish you'd told me that before. I'd have stood over her while she burned the lot. What's her number?'

'She isn't on the phone,' Helinger said. 'We could drive out, though.'

'I shan't be free until around lunchtime. That army major's coming again. He wants to agree the gist of my talk to his men.'

'Major Craythorne? The chap who walked in on us in the Computer Room?'

'That's him,' Westerly said. 'A bit of a peacetime soldier, I think. Don't know how he'd show up in a real battle.'

Peter Helinger's attention was diverted from his other worries. 'I bumped into him again at the Rotarians,' he said. 'Don't let the soft manner fool you. From what I've heard, he's a very tough nut. Decorated for going underground in Belfast and again after the Falklands. His colonel tries to keep him tucked away in the soft jobs because if he lets him near any action all hell's inclined to break loose. So the chairman told me.'

'Doesn't sound like the same chap,' Westerly said, 'but, just in case, I'll be careful what I say to him.'

'You do that,' Helinger said. 'I was wondering how much he heard, that day. You're sure he's bona fide?'

Westerly thought back for a few seconds before he replied. 'Quite sure,' he said. 'I've phoned him at the barracks. It was a coincidence. He only heard me sounding off about masterly inactivity, which is my recipe for almost any problem. I'll have to lunch the gallant major, I suppose.'

103

Dr Helinger was bored with college life after an endless academic year fraught with economic cuts and internal politics. The day was fine but humid. A trip into the country suddenly seemed like the prospect of Heaven. 'I'll take a run out,' he said. 'I want to discuss next year's programme with Polly and there are some books I want to return. You could follow me out when you're free.'

'My car's in dock. If I get through with the major before you're back, I might get him to drop me out there. It's not far out of his way back to camp. I can get a lift back with you. In case I don't manage,' Dr Westerly added, 'for God's sake get any papers off her and remind her not to do anything, say anything or even think anything until we're sure the shit's stopped coming down.'

'I'll do that,' Peter Helinger said.

'Mind you do. You can Bowdlerise the wording if you like, but don't leave anything out.'

The sunlit scenery, foreground sharp but with mist softening the contrasted tones as distance receded, might have delighted a painter; but the two men in the car were not in tune with the beauties of nature. They had soon run out of conversation about their few common interests. The car, standing in the unshaded road and without the benefit of a breeze, was becoming uncomfortably hot.

'He's been there over an hour,' Harry Moyes said suddenly.

Leo had already waited out a long prison sentence. An hour was no more than one tick of the clock. 'Searching takes time,' he said. 'Interrupt him and you'll only make it take longer.'

'I've got a feeling in my water that something's

wrong. For all we know, she's living with a feller. And there could be a path through the trees at the back. It looked to me as if he found the door open. That suggests that they're not far away.'

Leo thought about it. 'Nah,' he said. 'There'd have been jam sandwiches yodelling up to the door. And people don't lock doors much in the country.'

'Maybe,' Harry said. 'Maybe not. I'm going in. If he's alone and still searching, there's no harm done. It's all right for you, but that's my nephew in there. If anything happens to him, like being in a fight or getting nicked, I'll have my sister after my blood.'

Leo found the last argument more compelling. 'If you got to go, you got to go,' he said indulgently. 'But you want to learn patience.'

'At least it will get us out of this sweat-box.' Harry started the engine but then sat, irresolute.

Leo grunted in irritation. 'Come on, then. Let's go,' he said.

Harry set the car in motion. 'I always reckon that anyone who uses that expression doesn't know whether he's coming or going,' he grumbled.

'Who does, with you around?'

Harry halted the car near the mouth of the short drive. They got out and closed the doors gently. It was cooler near the trees. 'Barge straight in,' Leo said. 'If you ring, he'll bolt out the other side.'

'Right.'

They stepped as lightly as they could over the gravel. Harry opened the front door. A few paces took him along the passage to where he could see shadows moving on the kitchen wall. Leo crowded in behind him. Polly and Teeth looked up from a welter of papers. Teeth tried to make deterrent signals but he was too late.

105

'What goes on?' Harry asked him. 'You were for ever.'

Teeth saw Polly staring at him in shocked realisation and he knew that the game was over. 'You stupid old turds!' he said. 'I was getting the whole of it, no pain, no aggro, no sweat, and now you've buggered it up.'

Leo grunted angrily but Harry patted him on the shoulder. 'The boy's only blowing off steam,' he said. 'Let it go.'

'You were lying to me,' Polly said.

The boy found himself unable to meet her eye. 'I was trying to get what they want without you having to face them.'

'I thought better of you,' Polly said to Teeth.

'More fool you,' Harry said, and to Teeth, 'How far did you get?'

'I understand most of it,' Teeth said. 'Not the actual codes. But she's got some papers here in the house. She kept nipping out to look at them. Keep her here while I see what I can find.' He slipped out of the room, happy to escape from Polly's reproachful eyes.

'I'm going to get some clothes on,' Polly said.

Harry put his hand on her shoulder and kept her in her chair. 'Stay where you are,' he said. 'Unless you want us to come and keep an eye on you?'

Polly blinked back some unaccustomed tears. Teeth's unmasking had ended what was, to one of her innocent mind, an idyll. 'What right have you to tell me what to do? You're not from the bank. You're just a bunch of crooks.'

Leo had been standing well back from the awesome female, but he was not going to be insulted. 'That's the pot miscalling the kettle,' he said. 'You watch your tongue. Ever heard of the Hong Kong Property Development Trust?'

Polly deflated. 'Oh, that!' she said.

'Yes, that.'

'You still have to be a crook or you'd have gone to the police instead of chasing after us yourself,' she pointed out. 'So you're no better than I am.'

'Maybe not,' Harry said gently. 'In fact, he's a great deal worse. But he's bigger than you are and much, much angrier. So just sit quietly like a good girl and maybe you won't lose anything at all. He doesn't mind what you took out of the bank; it was the fact that you picked on his personal nest-egg that bugged him. It's no skin off your pretty little backside if he recoups himself for what you took off him from some other account.'

To Polly, whose conscience had already been nagging, this seemed almost reasonable. 'I want to get dressed,' she repeated.

'My dear, we prefer you as you are.'

Teeth returned, smiling. (Seeing the flash of his smile, Polly remembered too late the janitor's words.) He put a thick file of papers on top of the clutter on the table. 'This is it,' he said.

'You're sure?' Leo grunted.

'I don't know if it's enough, but it's the right file. The phone-number's here and a whole lot of codes, maybe all of them. If I could try them, I could soon tell.'

'Try them, then,' Leo said impatiently.

'On a computer.' In cold blood, Teeth did not dare to call Leo stupid again, but his tone implied it.

'Where—?'

They were interrupted. A car door slammed and there was a voice in the hallway. A lean figure appeared in the door. Leo stretched out a hand and jerked. Dr Peter Helinger shot into the room and fetched up against the cooker. The small kitchen was becoming very crowded.

Helinger's rolling eye found Polly. 'Who are these people?' he asked indignantly. 'What's going on?'

Harry tapped Polly lightly on the head. 'Tell him, darling.'

'They seem to be the Hong Kong Property Development Trust,' she said.

'Wrong,' said Leo. 'I'm the Hong Kong Property Development Trust. Just me, and don't any of you forget it. And you're the other genius who thought you could get away with embezzling a hundred and fifty thousand quid out of my account.' Helinger flinched. Leo rounded on Teeth. 'You want a computer?'

'Yes.'

'You.' Leo pointed at Polly while looking slightly over her head. 'Where's the nearest computer?'

'There's one in my living room. But it won't do you a damn bit of good.'

'Shut up. Go and look at it,' Leo told Teeth.

'She's right,' Teeth said. 'It's nothing like compatible. Anyway, there's no phone-line here.'

'What's more—' Polly began.

This time Leo met her eye, and what she saw in his stopped her dead. 'I told you to shut up,' he said, 'and I meant it.' He picked up a dishcloth. 'You want this between your teeth?'

Wide-eyed, Polly shook her head. Peter Helinger was trying to convey something to her by warning looks.

'Right, then.' Leo looked at Teeth. 'So what's next? We can't just go off with these papers and hope we've got it all, not even if these two creeps said that we had. We got to test it. Could we get into the Computer Room at the College overnight?'

Teeth shook his head emphatically. He had done his research as thoroughly as any member of the University. 'There's a security firm patrols with dogs. They phone the police if they see people or lights which they haven't been warned about. And that Computer Room's like a goldfish bowl.'

'That's enough problems,' Leo said. 'What I want is solutions.'

The room fell silent. Leo spoke again. 'The security firm wouldn't call the cops if this bloke went back to work at night, would they?'

'I'd guess not,' Teeth said. 'He's probably the one who tells them who's going to be working.'

'Then we'll send him in to do the whole job, keeping the girl as a hostage.'

'My dear ... chap,' Harry began. He had nearly committed the sin of using real names. 'We don't know that there's enough between them to guarantee his good conduct. Even if there is, he might well decide that her chances are better if he calls for help. In fact, what you're suggesting might be all that's needed to push him over the edge and send him running to the cops even if he had to confess his own sins. You fancy having the SAS busting in here?'

'I'm not giving up now,' Leo said. His tone belied his words.

'You don't have to,' Teeth said suddenly. 'I got a solution for you. There's one computer terminal in a building miles from anywhere and the staff are away on some consultancy job. We could use that. I could take the car and—'

'And draw a million or two for yourself and never come back,' Leo said. 'Thanks but no thanks. We'll all go.'

'Our car's hired for the day,' Harry said. 'If it doesn't go back today, somebody may get curious. We don't want it reported stolen.'

'He came in a car.' Leo pointed at Peter Helinger. Leo

was once again the leader, crisp and in command. 'And she probably has one in the shed. Take your pick. We'll go to wherever-it-is with two cars and then Gnashers can take your one back, collect Joe Soak in case we need him and get a taxi to the nearest crossroads. Except, maybe . . .' Leo pointed at Helinger again. 'Do we need him any more?'

Harry Moyes was the first to react to the implication. 'For Christ's sake, Leo,' he said, 'he can't say a word to anyone. None of them can. They've broken every law in the book.'

'There's no telling what somebody'll spill once the fuzz gets hold of them,' Leo said flatly. 'Remember what you said a minute back.'

One at a time, the others were catching on. Teeth's voice went up with fright. 'I never . . . I won't . . .'

'You'll do exactly what you're told,' Leo said.

Polly had caught a frantic look from Peter Helinger, whose eyes looked black in his blanched face. Anger over-rode fear. She sprang up, darted round Harry's stout body and faced Leo, a Fury defending her young. 'Don't even think such a thing or you'll never see a penny. If the bank has any sense, the codes have been changed. You'll need me and I can't manage without him. We're a team.'

Leo glared and his huge hands curled. Teeth, wondering what strange emotion was taking him over, prepared to rush in and grab for the gun which he knew was in Leo's waistband. But Leo was the first to look away. He pulled out Pepe Filbustini's Walther. 'Face the wall, both of you,' he said, 'and put your hands behind you. Gnashers, find the clothes-line.'

'I don't see why you can't give me my fifty and let me go,' Clem Pilling said. The glamour of close association

110

with one of the Filbustini brothers was fading rapidly. A long wait in the hired car had made it clear that the gangster had little conversation and was not given to changing his socks. Worst of all, Mark's physical presence seemed to emanate both power and evil.

'Because I may want some more help, that's why,' Mark said. 'You got some objection to earning more money?'

'No.' Clem would have liked to explain that, while he was happy to earn good money for going and watching and reporting, he was terrified of being drawn into the rough stuff. He was too young and too special to be put at risk. But that wasn't the sort of thing you said to the Filbustinis. 'What we going to do, then?' he asked.

It was a reasonable question. 'When Harry Fucking Moyes turns up,' Mark said, 'I don't want to top him here. Not if I don't have to. I want to get him in the car and take him somewhere we can talk. You can hold my gun on him. You can do that much, can't you, without letting it off? I've shown you how it works.'

'I can do that,' Clem agreed. 'But I wouldn't want him going and telling my mum I'd done it.'

'Believe me,' Mark said, 'he won't be telling your mum nothing.'

Clem found the comment less than comforting. He settled himself uneasily in the passenger seat and looked yet again at the garage a hundred yards away along the almost deserted street.

'You'll be all right,' Mark said. 'Anyway, you're all I got. So you better get it right or, maybe, next time I'm waiting for somebody it could be you. Savvy?'

'I'll get it right,' Clem said.

'Right. Let's go over it. If there's somebody with him—'

'There was somebody with him when he picked the

car up,' Clem said. 'A big man. Christ, he was big!'

The car moved on its springs as Mark jerked in his seat. 'You never said that before,' he said.

'Never knew it was important.'

'What did he look like, this other man?'

'Huge. He'd a head shaped like an oil-drum with a blob stuck on for a nose.'

'What else?'

'That's all I noticed. Except that he was big. Big all over.'

The more Mark thought about it the more sure he became that, while there might be other men in the country to fit that description, only one of them was likely to be getting into hired cars with Harry Moyes. Two con artists, each of whom had recently taken the Filbustinis for mugs; it couldn't be coincidence.

'This changes things,' he said. 'Unless Harry comes back with some big man I don't know, we leave him alone and follow.'

ELEVEN

Westerly walked down the stairs with his visitor. Major Craythorne was a tall but otherwise unremarkable young man with a retiring manner and an Old Etonian accent. When they had previously met, his tie had also been Old Etonian, but today he was in camouflaged battledress because, as he explained, he was homeward bound from an exercise.

Not even the martial trappings could make Craythorne look formidable. There was an athletic spring to his step, to be sure, but in all other respects he was typical of the chinless wonders whom Westerly had sometimes met on his rare ventures into society. Surely any resemblance between this man and the Craythorne described by Helinger could be no more than coincidence?

Westerly glanced sideways at his visitor and was surprised to see that he had a firm chin. The self-effacing manner obscured it.

At the foot of the stairs, they paused. 'That's fine,' Craythorne said. 'I think the wavelength's right. Not over the men's heads, but enough to make them think, those of them who are capable of it. I'm obliged to you.'

Hector Westerly made modest noises. He had entered

into discussion about his forthcoming educational talk to the soldiery already knowing that the talk would be the one which he gave, with minor variations, to Women's Institutes and Round Tables. 'If you're quite sure you won't lunch . . .' he said.

'Thank you, but no. My RSM's waiting patiently, but he might not remain patient indefinitely. When you do your thing, of course, I'll lunch you in the mess. I think you'll enjoy it. A lot of interesting chaps, and we do ourselves rather well.'

The sight of an open, olive-green Land-rover reminded Westerly of other matters. 'If you're sure you won't stay,' he said, 'perhaps I could beg a lift off you. It's almost on your route back to barracks.'

'By all means,' the major said cheerfully. 'It's a small return for plugging the gap in our educational programme. Take the front and I'll hop in the back. We can get three in the front but you need to know each other rather well, especially the driver and the man in the middle with the gear-leavers between his legs. This is RSM Heather. This, Sar'nt-major, is the eminent academic gentleman who's going to instil an understanding of international economics into the brutal and licentious, at the same time, I hope, showing us how to beat the current budgetary cuts. He bespeaks a lift. I think we can oblige him?'

'No trouble at all,' the RSM agreed. He was younger than Westerly had expected, smart and tough-looking. His sandy hair was cropped short.

The major vaulted lightly over the side of the Land-rover and settled himself in the back.

Westerly managed to keep up his end of the small talk as they drove, but he had only visited Polly at home on one occasion and on that trip he had been chauffeured by Peter Helinger. He had to search the dimmest

114

recesses of his memory to recall the way. He was not by nature a rural dweller and country roads all looked the same to him, but after only a few detours and the minimum retracing of steps he caught sight at last of the cottage from much the same viewpoint as that used earlier by Leo and Harry. There was an unfamiliar car near the gate.

'Would you stop, please?' he said suddenly.

Heather pulled up.

The Land-rover gave a higher viewpoint than a car so that gaps in the hedge were more plentiful. Westerly was granted a grandstand view of the loading and departure of two cars. These reached the road and turned away from them. 'Would you ... would you mind following those cars, at a distance?' he asked hesitantly. 'I'll explain in a minute.'

Without comment, RSM Heather slipped the Land-rover into gear. He stayed well behind the two cars and when a convenient van pulled out of a side-road he fell in behind it, observing the cars from behind its bulk. Westerly, distraught though he was, recognised that the RSM seemed to be experienced in surveillance. They seemed to be heading south, in the general direction of the river.

'Forgive my mentioning it,' the major said diffidently, 'but you might be wise to tell us what's wrong.'

'Wrong?'

'Wrong. Quite apart from being asked to shadow a pair of cars, which we would have found normal enough in Ulster but not in the British countryside, I'm not exactly blind. I saw what happened. And when a young lady, wearing outdoors only a dressing-gown which gapes at the front, keeps her hands clasped behind her back while getting into a car, even I can tell that something's amiss. One, and possibly two, of the five

115

people in those cars are reluctant passengers. Did I recognise your Computer Room boss – Dr Helinger?'

'You did.'

'What's more, one of the other men was armed. Is it a kidnapping?'

Dr Westerly strove desperately to think with his usual logic, but it seemed to have deserted him. 'Sort of,' he said.

'We could easily radio ahead for the police.'

'That would be disaster,' Westerly said.

'A worse disaster than a kidnapping?' Major Craythorne sounded only faintly surprised.

'Yes. No. Frankly, I don't know.'

'That much at least is self-evident. Don't you think you'd better tell us about it? The time seems to be past for the masterly inactivity which you were advocating when I walked in on you.'

They had descended from the rolling agricultural land and were headed seaward, parallel to the estuary coast. The estuary itself and the adjacent flood-plain, to their right, were hidden under a sea-mist and whenever their road dipped into the mist they were in danger of losing sight of the cars in front. The sergeant-major spurted and slowed and cursed under his breath and somehow maintained contact without, as far as they could tell, attracting attention.

Without quite knowing why, Hector Westerly found himself telling the whole story to the two soldiers, omitting little and even, as the mantle of the habitual public speaker fell over him, arranging it into anecdotal form.

'Let me see if I've got this straight,' Craythorne said at the end. 'Your university was running out of funds and jobs were threatened. So you three innocents breached the security of the National Bank and told its

116

computer to make a transfer of what you guessed to be hot money from a dormant account. You got away with it when the bank's investigators came round. But the gentlemen who have just carried off your two friends are not behaving like bank staff, nor yet like the police. They may therefore be presumed to be either the original depositors or some other crooks who have realised that you have the Midas touch.'

'That just about sums it up,' Westerly said.

Craythorne thought it over in silence. If the girl and the other man had not been in evident danger, it would have been devastatingly funny. Instead, he felt an upsurge of an old excitement. Life of late had been weary, stale, flat and unprofitable.

The RSM knew exactly what was going through the major's mind and he hid a smile. The two had worked together, on and off, for years, ever since they had been lieutenant and corporal together in Ulster. It would be his job to try to keep the mad bugger out of trouble or to clean up the subsequent mess. The trouble, he knew, was that when it came to the crunch he was capable of being as mad as his officer. One of these days they would come a cropper, the two of them.

He cursed suddenly and braked. The mist had been thin. Always it had looked as if visibility would be down to nil a few yards ahead but always that barrier had moved away in front of them. This time, suddenly, it was like running into a wall of milk. He could hardly see the sides of the road. He declutched and switched off, letting the Land-rover freewheel for a second. He could hear the car ahead still going. It must have somebody aboard who knew the road.

'Left-hander coming up,' said a voice beside him.

The RSM re-started his engine as the bend came at him.

They climbed out into thinner mist and then, after a mile or more, into clear air. There was no sign ahead of the two cars. Heather put his foot down and noise and wind battered at them. They topped a rise. The road ahead was empty as far as the next ridge.

RSM Heather pulled in to the side and stopped. 'Lost 'em,' he said. 'Shall I use the radio?'

'Not yet.' Major Craythorne leaned over the back of the seats. He had the map open in his hand. 'Is that Beasley Farm over there?'

'I think so,' Westerly said.

'Then we only passed two side-roads running inland, neither of them going anywhere much, and one which seems to angle down to the estuary. Any idea where they'd be going?'

'None at all,' Westerly said.

'Think,' Craythorne said urgently. 'What would they want. Somewhere lonely to hide prisoners?'

'The cottage would have done for that. I suppose they'd want . . . want . . .' It came to him so suddenly that he almost choked on his excitement. 'I've got it! Turn back and take it easy. I'll see if I can find the place again.'

After half a mile they left the road by way of a crude farm-track. Farmland gave way to sand and coarse grass. They stopped the Land-rover between wind-stunted trees. The dunes ahead seemed to be holding back the mist.

'I'm going to take a look,' Westerly said. 'If things seem as bad as I think they are, I'll have to call the police. You've been very good and I mustn't involve you any deeper, but if you could hang on a minute I may need the use of your radio or a lift to the nearest phone.'

'We're coming with you,' the major said firmly and

118

the RSM nodded. They descended from the Land-rover before he could argue.

Secretly relieved to have company and support, Westerly led the way through dunes and up a slight rise to the crest. Following the soldiers' example, he crawled the last few yards and looked through the fringe of reedy grass. His new summer suit would never be the same again.

The dunes fell away abruptly below them, down to the flood-plain. The mist, glowing in thin sunshine, lay low over the water, making it difficult to guess where the shore-line ran, but they were looking towards a building which stood out of the mist, seemingly at the very edge of the water. There was no sign of people, but they could see the two cars standing empty beside the building.

'What is this place?' the major asked, studying the scene through heavy binoculars.

'It used to be a lifeboat station,' Westerly explained. 'When they went over to inflatable inshore lifeboats we bought the place and extended it for use as an estuary research laboratory. The staff are away doing a consultancy job at Hull or Grimsby or somewhere.'

'Apart from its remoteness, what would the attraction be?'

'It has a phone-line,' Westerly said, 'and a terminal to the university computer.'

'All is explained,' Craythorne said. 'Hullo, there's activity.' A figure emerged from the building, settled into one of the cars and drove off slowly along the track which led to the main road. 'Damn! We could have intercepted him where they left the road.'

'We could still overtake him,' the RSM said hopefully.

Craythorne shook his head. 'We don't want any fun

and games where Joe Public may get uptight about it,' he said. 'This seems to be a nice, discreet sort of spot. We'll deal with them here.'

Leo Gunn opened the side door of the old lifeboat station by leaning his full weight against it and the party moved inside. A modern, single-storey block of offices and laboratories had been added on the landward side, but the main building, where they were, remained a single, large barn, stone-built, concrete-floored and slate-roofed, smelling of paint and tar and dampness. It was mainly a workshop and the winter home for the boat which was used for study trips to river and sea. Some of the floorspace was taken up by a winch and the converted lorry chassis which acted as the boat's trolley; the rest was bare except for a clutter of tools and equipment and a large inflatable dinghy standing vertically against the wall.

Harry and Teeth looked around them. Leo pushed his two captives against the wall and went to look through the doorway to the extension.

'This isn't going to work,' Helinger whispered.

'No.'

'Spin it out. I don't see them letting us go.'

'Nor do I,' Polly said. She was shivering uncontrollably, only partly due to the cold.

They waited, passively, for some unspecified change still to come. The pistol was out of sight but Leo's bare hands were too intimidating to allow any thoughts of resistance.

Leo grunted in disgust. 'Another bloody goldfish bowl. One person's enough in there, to keep watch.'

'I'll do it,' Teeth said.

'Nah. You wouldn't be able to keep your hands off the computer. I don't want you touching it unless I'm

120

looking over your shoulder and I want the approaches watched.' While he spoke, Leo was examining the odds and ends on a small workbench. 'Harry, go and watch for anyone taking an interest.'

'Right. I can't see much out there, though,' Harry said. 'It's getting thick.'

'You can see a hundred yards and more. Give me that much warning and nobody makes it in here in one piece. Here's what we want,' Leo said. He picked up four Jubilee clips, metal straps which could be tightened with a screwdriver, left over from some work on the boat's plumbing. 'Here, Gnashers. Make those two secure.'

Teeth was puzzled. 'They're already tied,' he said.

'Parcel string can be cut, frayed, burned or chewed,' Leo said. He was speaking as to a young man on the threshold of a new career. 'As for you two, do as you're told or we'll take the easy road and nail you to something.'

Teeth approached Polly respectfully and untied her wrists, waiting while she rubbed away the soreness and tidied her dressing-gown. Under Leo's directions, he put one clip on to her wrist, opened the other and threaded it through the first. Gently, he pulled her wrists back again.

'In front of her, you clown,' Leo said. 'Keep her away from screwdrivers and there's no way she can get loose. You want to have to feed her and wipe her bum? Don't answer that.'

Teeth did as he was told, linking her crossed wrists in front of her. He was as close to tears as was the girl. 'I'm sorry,' he whispered. 'Sorry. So sorry. Do what I can. Mayn't be much.'

'Tighter,' Leo snarled. 'Christ, if she sneezed they'd bloody fall off! Take up the slack.'

Teeth shrugged and went back to work.

When both prisoners were to Leo's liking, he made them stand with their backs against two of the uprights of the big boat's trolley. He cut two lengths of rope from a coil and, mistrusting the younger man's skill at ropework, himself attached the captives by their elbows. 'There you are, young Gnashers,' he said. 'Simple but effective. And if they make a nuisance of themselves, we just open the big doors and launch them down the slipway.'

Polly had resented being luggage but she had guarded her tongue. Being reduced to a fitment was too much for her control. 'You rotten shit-pig!' she burst out. 'Does it give you some sort of kick to terrorise . . . ?' She realised, almost too late, that a reference to innocent people might provoke another storm. 'Us?' she finished lamely.

Leo put his face close to hers but he could hear those damning voices in the hiss of the water pipes and the screech of the gulls outside. Unwilling to meet her eye, he focused on the bridge of her nose.

'You got off lightly so far,' he said. 'Now I'll tell you something. But not in front of a witness,' he added. He took three steps sideways and flicked with his fist. The blow seemed casual, but Peter Helinger slumped, supported only by his elbows. Leo returned to Polly.

'Not long back,' he said coldly, 'when I found out my money'd gone, I thought my lady-friend'd done it. When I'd finished with her, I left her tied to a door. I guess she's been dead for weeks by now. You could say that she died for your sins. Think about it before you say anything you might regret. All right?' There was a silence. 'I said, all right?' He took hold of the neck of Polly's dressing-gown.

The threat was enough. 'All right,' she said quickly.

She found that her shivers had become a shake which set the whole trolley aquiver.

Leo turned away. As far as he was concerned, the matter was finished. 'I forgot about you,' he told Teeth. 'You can just forget you heard anything. But, any time you feel like talking about it, just remember the message. Got it?'

Teeth nodded and looked away.

'Good. Now we can get on. Your Uncle Harry can take the car back and fetch Joe Soak while you have a first try at the computer. I'll keep watch.'

'This may take some time,' Teeth said.

'We've got time. And you got some skilled help, slightly damaged. Harry can bring some grub back with him.'

Westerly and the two soldiers had moved further along the dunes to the highest point, from which they could better observe, through a screen of reedy grass, the approach track and the entrance to the building.

The doctor was beginning to fume with nervous impatience. Craythorne set out to soothe his fears. 'Your pals are safe for the moment,' he said, without lowering his binoculars. The mist was low over the water and most of the building stood sharply above it. 'They wouldn't have been brought along at all if the need for their help wasn't foreseen, and nobody's going to knock them off until it's certain that they've outlived their usefulness. And it's all going to take time. But if we do anything too precipitate, they may turn from assets into hostages and then we might have a real problem.'

'You don't understand,' Westerly said. He shifted his position. Sand and stiff grass did not make a comfortable couch. 'It may not take long to find out that there's no way anybody's going to get access to the bank's computer again.'

'That's a pity,' Craythorne said lightly. 'I was rather looking forward to upping my permitted overdraft. Why not?'

'They've probably changed all the codes. But the first thing the bank would have done, the moment they suspected anything wrong, would have been to change the phone-number for the central computer. We only found the original one by accident.'

'The new one couldn't be found by trial and error?'

'Even allowing for digits which are reserved for service functions, I'd guess that there would be around nine thousand possible numbers. At, say, two a minute—'

'You've made your point,' Craythorne said. 'So we won't hang about. But one thing the army taught me was that time spent on reconnaissance is seldom if ever wasted. If you delay you may miss a chance, but if you rush in you will quite definitely blow it. Your friends should be bright enough to stall for a while. Have you been inside the building?'

'Often. I was on the steering committee.'

'Good. Describe the layout in as much detail as you can remember. Try not to point – there's somebody looking out from the windowed bit and we're on the skyline.'

Westerly concentrated. 'The large building is one big shed with high windows,' he said. 'You can see the usual entrance.'

'The door looks a bit second-hand. Somebody seems to have kicked it in.'

'One would suppose so. At the far end there are big sliding and folding doors. You can just make out the top of the slipway.'

'Got it,' Craythorne said. 'Is there a wicket in the big doors?'

'As far as I remember, yes. There's a single doorway leading through into the extension, which has no external doors of its own. You go through a short corridor with lavatories one side and a utility room on the other. As you can see, the extension is mostly window. From left to right as we look at it, you've got Biochemistry Lab, Sedimentation Lab, office and a workshop for the instrumentation. The computer's in the office, which is where that chap's sitting.'

'He may be trying the computer,' Craythorne said, 'and much good may it do him, but he's also keeping an eye on the approaches. What about the roofs below us?'

'Just a pair of cottages, once occupied by the lifeboat crew. They're used as stores.'

RSM Heather cleared his throat. 'There's no easy approach,' he said. 'Not under cover. I was wondering ... There's a mast sticking up out of the mist, away to the right.'

Craythorne turned his binoculars that way. 'You're right,' he said. 'Looks like the top of the mast of a small sailing-boat.'

'Jim Warden, the scientific officer, keeps his own boat on a mooring there,' Westerly said.

'Perfect,' said Craythorne. 'I was wondering how to get close without being spotted. It looked like a water-borne job, but I wouldn't back myself to swim that far, not with the amount of gear I'll have to carry. The ebb's started to run by now. I can drift down.'

'They'll see the mast moving,' Westerly objected.

'Not a chance. The windows don't look towards the water, and people can be extraordinarily blind to what's happening beyond the shore-line.' Craythorne looked up at the sky. When he spoke again it was clear that he had gathered his thoughts. 'Fortunately, we're not short of equipment. We were carrying most of the spares for a practice assault on a hilltop. We'll fetch what we need from the Land-rover and then I'll go in on my own.'

'Beg pardon,' Heather said, 'but I think I should be with you.'

'So do I,' Craythorne said. 'But you'll be more useful as backup. If the top blows off, you can get to me in under thirty seconds.'

Heather nodded. 'Orders, Major?'

'No orders. Use your discretion. I'd have liked to have you intercept any visitors, but I don't see how you can stop a car without inviting the attention of the police. We've nothing to make a road-block. No trees to fell—'

'The body of a man lying in the roadway?' the RSM suggested. The two soldiers looked at Westerly.

'No, thank you very much,' Westerly said. 'I want to do all I can, but I've got to draw the line somewhere. They might not feel much like stopping.'

Craythorne grunted. That was the trouble of working with civilians. Unlike soldiers, they had no sense of their own expendability. 'So we'll manage without a road-block,' he said. 'We'll use the radios. Keep me posted. Bear in mind that there are dozens of sets with similar crystals; what's more, a sudden squawk could alert the enemy, so use Morse if you can, the way we did it in 'Derry. We saw four men and a girl get into the cars. We've seen one man drive off. The girl and one man are prisoners. If you see the other two men and neither of the prisoners in the glazed offices, tell me quickly – it'll be my chance to get them out. What have I forgotten?'

The RSM thought about it. 'Damn-all, sir,' he said.

* * *

Leo Gunn stood in the short corridor between the lifeboat shed and the extension. He found that he could see through the open door to watch his prisoners in the dim shed and also in the other direction, into and through the extension, observing Teeth as he wrestled in prayer with a computer which, if not defunct, seemed to be in need of Intensive Care. At the same time, Leo could overlook a broad sweep of grass and sand until it vanished in the mist, without showing himself to the outside world.

Peter Helinger stirred and groaned. He was first conscious of the pain in his elbows. He found some strength in his quaking legs and took his own weight. About the pain in his head and jaw he could do nothing. Looking groggily around, recognising where he was and remembering the danger, he groaned more loudly. Leo ignored the sound.

The staff of the estuary research laboratory had embarked in some haste in order to catch a tide and nobody had thought to turn off the water at the mains. As a result, the urinal in the male toilet still regularly flushed itself, and the cistern over Leo's head constantly refilled with a steady hiss. Leo was hardly aware of the noise, but a few tentative words soon convinced Polly Holt that it would be safe to converse in whispers.

'Are you all right?' Polly wanted to know.

'No,' Helinger whispered back. He gave the vital question some more thought. 'I'll survive . . . I think. I talked you into this mess. I'm sorry.'

The past was of no interest to Polly. 'Forget it. What's going to happen?' she asked.

Helinger struggled to make his brain function. 'Who knows? It doesn't look good, but any one of a dozen things could happen, given long enough. Somebody may come. The staff of this place might come back.

Westerly may call the police. Listen, after they find out they can't dial through, we must stall.'

'Watch it,' Polly whispered. She was close to tears but her brain surprised her by working in top gear, balancing logic against logic in neat array. 'That boy knows too much to be blinded easily with science. Keep thinking up sound technical angles.'

'I'll try, when my head stops behaving like a merry-go-round. Meantime, we must try to give fate a hand. Can you get loose?'

Polly wriggled. 'Not a chance.'

'Nor me. I've a lighter in my pocket, but the rope's behind me and my hands are in front. If he goes out, could we move the whole trolley over to the bench?'

'The wheels are blocked.'

'Sod it!'

In the office, Teeth was also driven into bad language. 'What's wrong?' Leo asked.

Teeth stretched, joints cracking. 'I been on to the University's computer once, but when I tried to move on to the number for the bank I got cut off.' (The two prisoners exchanged an anguished glance.) 'So I tried the University again, but the bloody number's always engaged.'

'Keep trying,' Leo said. 'It'll clear.'

'I don't know. This may be the day they run the payroll program or some such thing.'

Polly, Helinger noticed, was struggling to fray the rope at her elbows against the timber upright of the trolley. For his own part, he decided that her efforts were doomed. The rope was too thick, the post too smooth and, even if she succeeded, what good would it do her?

But he had no intention of waiting passively for death. If he must go, he would take that cantankerous

128

man-mountain with him.

The space beneath the trolley had become the accepted place for depositing tools and stores which had no other home. Peter Helinger studied the clutter, searching for some weapon which could be manoeuvred into his hands. There was a can of petrol for the outboard motor within reach of his feet. He wondered whether he could set the place on fire and with what result.

Jonathan Craythorne jogged upstream behind the dunes until he guessed that he was hidden from the old lifeboat station. He crossed the open in dead ground with the mist, thickest near the chill of the water, closing around him. The boat's mast, he estimated, was now fifty yards to his left. He paced off forty and then took to the water, swimming with difficulty and letting the ebb-tide carry him down. His more vulnerable equipment was sealed in a plastic bag in his haversack and the trapped air helped to offset the weight of gear, but if he had miscalculated he stood a good chance of drowning.

The hull of the sturdy, open sailing-boat showed black through the mist when he was almost past and he had to struggle to reach it. He hung on to the rudder until he had his breath . He was careful to climb over the stern but, even so, the mast must be signalling his arrival in the clear air above. He could only hope that no-body capable of reading the signs was looking that way.

Water squelched in his boots as, with a mental apology to the boat's owner, he made his way forward. Army boots are not acceptable footwear in cared-for boats. On the other hand, it did not seem that this particular owner was so fussy. All was in good order, but no effort had been made to impress. Spit, yes, he said to himself, but polish, no.

The boat was attached to a permanent mooring, but there was an anchor and warp aboard. He lashed the helm over with a spare sail-tie, dropped the mooring and lowered the anchor until it was no more than brushing the bottom. Under the combined influences of tide, rudder and the drag of the anchor the boat moved steadily downstream and at the same time angled shoreward.

The old lifeboat station showed up suddenly just as he was thinking that he had drifted too far and, at almost the same moment, the boat nudged stern-first into the slipway. Jonathan lifted the anchor. The tide would hold her.

He stepped on to the slip and moved cautiously up the slimy slope to the big doors. The fit was good at the joins and at the bottom, but he thought that his shadow might be seen from inside. The wicket door had a Yale lock, but there might be bolts. He settled himself against the stone jamb.

While listening for sounds from beyond the big doors, he opened his small haversack and the water-proof bag inside it. The radio seemed to be undamaged. He felt more at home with his revolver restored to its holster. The wetness of his uniform was of no importance. He had often experienced far worse conditions in the SAS. And at least there was no wind. In the Falkland Islands, this would have been considered luxury.

'He's aboard,' said RSM Heather.

'How do you know?'

'The mast's moving.'

Westerly realised that the mast was indeed close. 'He's quite a character,' he said. 'Do you know him well?'

'We've been together most of twelve years now,'

Heather said. 'Started as subaltern and corporal. I could tell you some stories. I won't, but I could.'

'If he manages to ... do something, what happens afterwards? Will he go to the police?'

A smile touched the corner of the RSM's mouth as he remembered the past. 'Not unless he has to,' he said. 'If he has to, he was going to all along. See what I mean?'

Westerly thought about it and found some comfort.

A puff of breeze from seaward banked the mist up for a minute. 'We could get down to those cottages,' Westerly said.

'We're better up here where we can see over the top.'

The breeze dropped. The mist subsided again. The mast came to rest opposite the corner of the building. It waggled once and then was still. Two minutes later the RSM's radio emitted a muffled sound as Jonathan Craythorne drummed his fingernails on his microphone. Heather replied in similar manner. 'Radio contact re-established,' he said to Westerly.

'You'd better tell him that somebody's coming,' Westerly said.

Heather twisted his head. 'You're right,' he said. He called up a mental picture of the Morse code and began to tap and stroke the microphone. The old patterns soon came back to him.

T-W-O M-E-N A-F-O-O-T S-H-A-L-L W-E S-T-O-P—?

The answer came back immediately. I-G-N-O-R-E.

They waited and watched. A lone shelduck flew over, calling. It seemed to be laughing at them.

Teeth shut down the computer terminal and left the room. 'Everything functions,' he told Leo. 'I can get through as far as the University mainframe, but the bank's phone-number comes up unobtainable.'

Peter Helinger had been trying to unscrew the lid of the petrol-can with his toes. He heeled it back to where it was half-hidden by his legs. He inserted his foot as far as it would go back into his shoe. It was the best that he could do.

'What d'you reckon?' Leo said.

'I want to ask one of them a question.'

Teeth tried to slip past but Leo stopped him with one finger. 'Tell me.'

Teeth met Polly's eyes and shrugged helplessly. 'She must have written the phone-number in code,' he said. 'I've tried the number as she wrote it down, and with one added to each digit and with one subtracted, and for all the good I did I might as well have tried scratching my bum. If it's code, she must have used something more complicated.'

Leo stalked across the floor, as cold as a glacier, as slow and as unstoppable. He stopped in front of Polly and opened her dressing-gown. With her elbows tied back, there was nothing she could do to resist. Leo put his hand in his pocket and pulled something out. There was a sharp click and a thin, blue-black blade appeared on the instant, as though it had always been there.

Teeth scampered after him, dwarfed in his shadow. 'Don't do nothing like that,' he squeaked.

'Bugger off,' Leo told him. The point of the knife touched her nipple. 'You got one chance,' he said, 'and it won't last long.'

Teeth braced himself for a suicidal attack. Beyond the big doors Jonathan Craythorne damned his luck. If only he could see ... Even as he reached for his radio he knew that there was no time to waste on orders to the RSM. Leo's voice had left no doubt that he was on the point of killing and the click had sounded like the cocking of a gun. Men coming or not, unready as he was, he had to go in now. He took two stun grenades from his haversack and drew his heavy revolver. He got to his feet and prepared for a sprint.

Polly's mind and tongue were paralysed with fear. It was Peter Helinger who found a voice which was both hoarse and shrill with nerves. 'You can't dial out from here,' he said. 'You can only connect to the University mainframe. Somebody at the mainframe has to connect you with the outside computer.'

Everything stopped. After a long moment, without removing his blade, Leo glanced at Teeth. 'Could that be true?' he gritted.

Teeth shrugged. 'It figures,' he said.

'Any way we could fix it by phone from here?'

'I don't see how,' Teeth said. 'We got the boss here. Even if there's a technician in the room, which I wouldn't bet on, an' we made his boss phone up, he'd wonder why the call was coming from here while the staff's away; see what I mean?'

Craythorne settled himself again. He wanted to pick his moment and to be sure that his back was safe.

Leo snapped his knife closed and dropped it into his pocket. 'When this is over, I'm going to have you,' he told Polly. He looked at Teeth. 'That's gives us one chance. Tonight, after things have settled down, you go . . .' There was a pause. 'No, not you. We need you here. That uncle of yours visits the college. Could you tell him exactly what to do?'

'I guess so,' Teeth said. 'We could always speak again on the phone if he's not sure.'

'That's how we'll play it, then.' Leo turned away from Polly, leaving her exposed. 'You write down for him every single step he has to take.'

He turned away. Teeth hesitated in front of Polly. He put out his hand and pulled the front of her dressing-

133

gown closed. His hand brushed her breast. They breathed out in unison. 'I'll do what I can,' he whispered. She nodded. Leo was watching so he had to turn away.

Outside in the cold mist, Jonathan Craythorne braced himself. When the two newcomers were inside he would follow them up.

The radio under his hand was emitting its soft clicks and hisses again. C-A-R C-O-M-I-N-G D-O-W-N.

He decided again to wait. How many more could the building hold?

TWELVE

Ted Hancock had reached the plateau of his alcoholic mountain. From this point on he would lose no more faculties, but there would be no return to sobriety except through the vale of delirium. When Harry Moyes helped him through the broken side door of the old lifeboat station, he was having difficulty in deciding which foot should go first.

Harry sat him down on a box of spares. Ted looked at Polly, blinked and looked away, disbelieving. The hallucinations were taking an unusual turn.

'All right?' Leo asked.

'I think so,' Harry said. 'Difficult to be sure we weren't followed, in this mist. The taxi-driver wouldn't douse his lights. I can't say I blamed him, but who'd be bothering?'

'If anyone's followed you, they'll be the ones that'll be bothered,' Leo said. 'Gnashers, stop looking at the bird unless you want me to think you're going to change sides.'

'I wouldn't do that,' Teeth said sullenly. 'I don't let mates down. Just a minute,' he added. 'I hear a car. No, it's gone now. Probably it was on the road.'

'So take this and keep an eye out the door.'

Avoiding the sight of Polly, Teeth gingerly accepted the Walther from Leo and walked to stand in the doorway. Harry glanced at the two captives without interest. 'Made any progress?' he asked.

'There's a snag,' Leo told him. 'We can't get through to the bank from here. Those two say that the machine here had to be put through by the big one, and Gnashers says it figures. You'll have to go to the Computer Room, after the cleaners are out, and dial the number from there.'

'I don't know nothing about computers,' Harry said unhappily.

Outside, Craythorne's radio was whispering again. A-R-M-E-D M-A-N I-N D-O-O-R. T-W-O W-A-T-C-H-I-N-G F-R-O-M T-R-A-C-K. S-H-A-L-L T-A-K-E T-H-O-S-E—?

His reply was short. G-O. He hoped that the new arrivals were not the police. RSM Heather could play rough at times.

'Nothing to it,' Teeth said over his shoulder. 'I'll write it all out for you, with pictures of where the switches are. There's a manual here ...' He faced into the shed and looked at his uncle. 'You'll have no problem, honest. A whole heap of evening research goes on, so there's a gap of hours between the last cleaner leaving and the locking-up by the janitors?'

Harry was far from satisfied.

'Suppose it's only that she's written the phone-number down in code or something?'

'We thought that,' Leo said. 'She says not and she knows I'll cut her tits off if she's lying.'

'If it's so easy, why can't Teeth go and do the whole job from there?' Harry asked.

'You go,' Leo said as if that settled the matter. Then he relented. 'Look, it's the difference between two

136

minutes to make the connection and what could be an hour or two to do the job. And Gnashers may need these two mugs handy to answer questions.'

'That's right,' Teeth said, his back to the door. He swallowed nervously. 'But I don't like this talk about cutting . . .'

'Oh, you don't?' Leo's tone was mildly amused.

Teeth drew himself up. 'No, I don't. And I won't let it happen,' he said shrilly.

'How you going to stop it?'

Teeth made a faint gesture with the pistol. Leo walked slowly towards him. Teeth, his breath snatching, brought up the Walther. Leo was towering above him before he could force himself to pull the trigger. The pistol clicked. Leo waited while he looked down at the safety-catch and tried to work the slide.

Leo took the pistol out of his hands. 'Think I'd give you a loaded gun?' he asked. 'I just wanted to know whose side you were on. And now I found out.' Suddenly, so quickly that the trembling boy never saw it coming, Leo punched him in the mouth. Teeth went down hard.

Two hundred yards away, RSM Heather came out from behind the cover of a dune to find that his quarry had moved on and would already be in view from the doorway. He turned and ploughed back through the sand between the dunes, gasping and swearing under his breath. Jonathan Craythorne, seeing the two dark shapes materialising out of the mist, tucked himself back behind the corner of the building. He would let them get inside before he moved. If he failed to catch all the participants in one grab, all hell could break loose.

Leo took the magazine out of his pocket and slapped it into the Walther, tucking the pistol back into his waistband. 'Now that we got that straightened out, you want to make anything of it?' he asked Harry.

Harry shrugged. 'He was out of line,' he said. 'You taught him all he needs to know. I'll forget it if you will. All the same, I'm not happy with this university caper. I don't know what I'm doing and I don't like leaving you two together.'

'You go,' Leo said, 'or you're out.'

'He's not going anywhere,' Mark Filbustini said, appearing in the doorway. 'Hullo, Harry.' Mark had a large automatic pistol in his fist and a brittle smile on his face. He stepped over Teeth and gave Harry a push in the back which sent him spinning across the floor. Clem Pilling emerged from the mist and entered nervously behind him. Mark's quick glance passed chillingly over the two captives as being of interest but no importance. 'Good to see you again, Leo.'

Leo looked at the Walther. 'You got shares in the Carl Walther Waffenfabrik?' he asked coldly. At the same time he tried to nudge his jacket over the pistol in his waistband.

Mark was not deceived. 'We bought a case of them,' he said. 'Fell off the back of a lorry. Junior, you check them for weapons. Don't get in the way.'

Jonathan Craythorne made ready to slip down from the platform at the head of the slipway and begin a cautious approach to the side door. He decided to wait for a count of thirty. If no more surprises emerged from the mist his moment might be approaching, while the parties were distracted by friction between themselves. Then, he might take them by surprise. Otherwise, there would undoubtedly be knife and bullet wounds and some very difficult questions to answer.

Very cautiously, Clem did as he was told, relieving Leo of the weight of the Walther. Harry, Teeth and the comatose Ted Hancock were unarmed.

'Right,' Mark said. 'Guard the door.'

Leo was not usually impressed by pistols. He was too big to be stopped by one shot from any handgun of less than magnum bore, and strong enough to kill before a second shot was fired. So nobody ever pulled a trigger on him at close range. But Mark was not the type to die quickly and so might reason differently.

'What the hell do you want?' Leo asked.

'You,' Mark said. 'And him,' pointing the pistol at Harry.

Major Craythorne's radio came alive. D-O-O-R G-U-A-R-D-E-D A-G-A-I-N it said. He gave himself a mental kick for dallying and took up his radio. D-I-S-T-R-A-C-T.

His radio replied, Y-O-U F-I-R-S-T. He nodded. It made sense. The RSM would need to come closer. He slid down off the slipway on the safe side.

Leo had no great fondness for Harry; but Teeth's usefulness was not yet over and might cease altogether if he saw his uncle thrown to the wolves. 'You can't have him,' Leo said shortly.

'No?'

Harry was not one to remain passive while his future was discussed. He pulled his wits together and found a reedy voice. 'Wouldn't you rather have your money back . . . several times over?' he asked.

Mark was more interested in the excuse to vent his feelings. 'You got that sort of money?' he asked disbelievingly.

'Come in with us and you can have ten times your money back,' Harry said. 'It's help-yourself time.'

This was different. 'How?' Mark asked.

Stumbling over words in his haste, Harry spilled out a summary. 'All we need now,' he finished, 'is one of us to visit the Computer Building and give us a connection

139

to the National Bank mainframe.'

Craythorne found three stones. He threw them, one at a time, far out into the water. RSM Heather saw Clem's head turn towards the splashing sounds and he was off, skittering down the face of the dune and into the cover of one of the old cottages. He placed his radio handy and searched around for a few stones of his own.

Mark Filbustini was thinking it over. Harry's proposition was attractive. The silence was broken by a strange, whinnying sound. Ted Hancock was laughing his head off.

For some reason, Mark took the laughter as a personal affront. He walked over and cuffed the side of Hancock's head. 'What's the joke? And it'd better be funny.'

The blow seemed to clear the fumes from Ted's brain but he was still laughing. 'First I've heard about not being able to dial out from the terminal,' he said thickly. 'Doesn't sound right. My bet is, they've changed the number. Issued new Autodiallers to branches. 'S what I'd do.'

'How do we get the new number?' Leo asked.

Ted shrugged and nearly fell over. 'Can't,' he said. 'Thousands and thousands.'

There was another moment of silence while rage built on fury in two men, to the point where it could be heard and smelled, and three people saw the face of approaching death.

RSM Heather threw a stone with all his might. It carried halfway to the building but pitched on sand. Its sound was lost.

Mark held his pistol pointed at Leo. 'If anyone tries to interfere,' he said, 'I'll blast him.' He fixed his eyes on Harry, who backed until stopped by solid wall.

Once the killing started, Polly knew who would be

140

next. The realisation gave wings to her mind and tongue. 'Even if he's right,' she said, 'we can still get the number. Electronically.' She hardly cared whether what she said made sense. Anything to postpone the evil moment.

As Leo began to relax, Mark Filbustini shook his head. 'I don't buy it,' he said. 'This man dies.'

Leo nodded. Teeth's usefulness, and therefore that of Harry, seemed to be over. 'I'll make you a present of him,' he said. He was on his toes, awaiting his chance.

'Thanks a bundle,' Mark said. 'And you're next.'

Leo refused to show fear. 'Like last time?'

'Don't count on it.'

Heather's next stone clicked gently on its second bounce. Clem glanced that way without curiosity. He was more interested in the activity in the shed, ready at any moment to take flight or to rejoin Mark Filbustini and share the jubilation, whichever offered him the better prospect of survival or reward at the time.

Teeth, blood pouring over his chin, had dragged himself to his feet. With more courage than sense, he staggered to his uncle's aid and was bowled over by a single back-handed blow. Mark took Harry by the throat, gently. He wanted this to last. He was enjoying himself. And there was still Leo to come.

Leo saw what might be his last chance and put all his agility into a jump for the gun.

It was a race which lasted for less than a second, a race between Leo's rush and Mark's reaction. The result was as near to a draw as it could be. Leo took a hasty bullet which passed through his left shoulder, glancing off his collar-bone. The impact span him round and he crashed backwards, all twenty stone of him, into Filbustini.

Outside in the mist, crouched in the angle between the slipway and the building and peeping round its corner, Craythorne heard the shot and knew that the moment had come. But although the man – no, the youth – with the automatic pistol was peering into the shed, he was also facing towards the shore. Sudden movement would catch his peripheral vision and alert him. The major reckoned the odds on a race round three sides of the building and discarded them.

During the collision, Mark Filbustini had suffered a heavy foot on his instep and a flailing arm had caught his wrist. The Walther flew out of his hand, fired once on landing and skidded to a stop by Polly's foot.

Heather's fourth stone was already on its way when the first shot sounded. It landed flat on another stone, sounding for all the world like a careless footfall and distracting Clem Pilling from the fight inside. He span round. Jonathan Craythorne began his run, silent on the sand.

Leo's left arm was useless but one arm would suffice. He grabbed Mark by the shoulder and prepared to butt. Mark, suddenly aware of Leo's strength, got his blow in first, a chop to Leo's shoulder. The bullet wound alone would not have stopped Leo, but the chop found his cracked collar-bone and the flare of pain sent him reeling against the wall.

Mark dived after his pistol. Polly kicked it away. She meant it for Teeth, but her aim was bad. It went under the workbench in the corner and buried itself in a mixture of sawdust and shavings.

Mark knew that, even if he could recover his pistol, it would be unlikely to fire again until the sawdust had been cleaned out of it. And Leo was between him and the corner. He looked at Polly under half-lowered lids. 'Right, girl,' he said. 'I'm going to have you when this is over.'

Polly closed her eyes.

Mark lifted his voice. 'Clem. Bring that other shooter in here.'

But Clem was lying unconscious at the major's feet with a broken wrist. He had been taken out in expert silence.

Jonathan Craythorne heeled the Walther into the sand. He lifted his radio to signal the RSM, but at that moment it spoke with terrible volume and clarity. 'You there, 'Arry?' it said. 'Where the 'ell you got to? You better get your arse back to HQ. You're wanted.'

Craythorne wasted no time in cursing the errant soldier whose misuse of the radio must have given warning to the enemy. His training took over. His hands were at work while his brain was still shuffling his options into their priorities. He bought time and distraction with a stun grenade thrown high through the door, snapped 'Come' into his radio before dropping it, and went through the door fast and low with his revolver in his hand.

The big shed was still echoing to the reverberation of the grenade and fragments of bakelite were pattering down. The reek of explosives hung in the air.

In an instant of appraisal, Craythorne saw that no guns were in view. Teeth was up again but half-stunned, Harry was down and holding his throat, Ted Hancock was drooping against the wall and Leo, who had been nearest to the grenade's blast, was reeling. Peter Helinger and Polly Holt, he saw at a glance, could be discounted. Mark Filbustini, coming at him with his hands outstretched and a crazed look in his eye, was the only immediate threat.

Reminding himself again that in soft, civilian circles bullets provoke questions requiring answers, Craythorne dropped his revolver smoothly into its holster. Mark grinned hugely. At last he had an

143

adversary, somebody whom he could pound and smash and tear. He came in with a rush.

Craythorne ducked under a punch which could have felled a horse. His training had taught him to kill rather than to subdue, but corpses would be less than convenient. As he danced aside he struck once, straight-fingered, for the solar plexus. It would have folded up most men, but Filbustini took it, half-winded but grinning. He seemed to have found an opponent worthy of his talents. He growled and bored in again, hands lower. Craythorne had time for one chop to the side of the neck before being gathered up in a bear-hug which threatened to crack his ribs. He held his breath, kneed for the groin and at the same time felt for the other's carotid arteries, and dug in his thumbs. After a few seconds, the crushing grip weakened and fell away and Filbustini went down on his knees. Craythorne released the other's neck, delivered a double-handed clap to the ears and finished with a knee which bowled the man over backwards.

Heather appeared in the door with Dr Westerly behind him. The RSM held a submachine-gun one-handed but at the ready, and with his other hand he proffered Jonathan's radio. 'You may be wanting this again, sir,' he said.

'I may indeed.' The major took a look around while snatching a few quick breaths. Everything seemed to be under control, except . . . The wicket in the big doors to the slipway was open, admitting mist and daylight. Leo's vast bulk had vanished and where Polly had stood there was only a length of rope draped over the launching-trolley.

Polly heard herself scream when Leo came at her with his knife out, but he was not after her blood. In the

144

sudden chaos and the disintegration of his plans, Leo saw her as a last link with his vanished hoard and his key to the vault of the National Bank. He slashed the rope which attached her by the elbows to the launching-trolley, dropped the open knife into his pocket and hauled her away.

All the action seemed to be between him and the side door. Leo had already marked the wicket in the big doors at the head of the slipway. He released her for a second while he unbolted and pulled it open and then dragged her through on to the platform. All eyes and ears were on the fighting.

One quick look round the corner of the shed was enough. There was no car in sight and two men were emerging from the mist and racing over the thin grass, one of them armed and ready to shoot.

On the other side, there was only mist and desolation.

But at the bottom of the slipway was a boat, not even moored but held against the slip by the ebbing tide. He pulled Polly, stumbling, down the slippery slope and tumbled her over the side. A quick glance behind showed no pursuit. He pushed off, boarding in the same movement. The wrench made his shoulder scream at him, but Leo had learned to ignore pain. Within seconds, the lifeboat station was lost to sight and sound.

They were alone in a calm, white world. All sense of time or direction was smothered. Leo lowered himself on to the gunwale, causing even that heavy boat to heel dangerously, nursed his shoulder and tried to gather his thoughts. Polly pulled herself on to the after-thwart and arranged her dressing-gown modestly around her. She had her own thoughts to gather.

When she felt that enough time had passed, and with it the danger of a nervous explosion, she asked, 'Can you swim?'

145

'Not a stroke. Shut up. Why d'you ask?' Leo added. His face was grey and sweating but the bleeding seemed to have stopped.

'We'll be down on some rocks if we don't get this boat under control soon.'

Leo might never have had to do with sailing-craft during his years at sea, but he knew about tides.

'That's right,' he said. 'Where's the motor?'

'No motor. You'll have to sail.'

That again made sense. The breeze was faint but to Leo, in his inexperience, it seemed enough. Fumbling with the unfamiliar gear, he uncovered and untied the mainsail which was already laced to its boom and yard.

'If you took these things off my wrists,' Polly said, 'I could help. I've sailed in this boat.'

But Leo was not prepared to have his prisoner, and a woman at that, loose in a confined space with him. 'You stay as you are,' he said gruffly. 'You can steer like that. Just tell me how this goes.'

'It's a gunter lug,' she said. 'Take the peak halliard off its cleat – starboard side of the mast.' Under her patient direction, he hoisted the large mainsail and sheeted it in. If he ignored the pain, he could get some use of his left hand. The boat heeled slightly and ghosted ahead. Water gurgled under the stem. Polly brought her round.

'Where do you think you're going?' Leo demanded.

'Just getting away from the rocks,' she said. 'Where do you want to go?'

Leo had been wondering the same thing and had decided that his first need was for a car. 'Make upstream as far as the first bridge,' he said.

'Aye aye, Skipper,' Polly said, more cheerfully than she felt. She brought the boat closer to the wind.

'I don't want anywhere crowded, mind,' Leo said. 'Is it quiet there?'

146

'Quiet as a graveyard,' Polly said. The most seaward of the bridges was a constantly bustling throng of pedestrians and cars, but she was safe for as long as Leo could envisage a way out.

Sailing was the only sport on which Polly had ever lavished any of her precious time. The intricate mathematical problems had suited her intellect, and she had been a welcome crew-member on several boats because of her ability to solve complex navigational equations in her head.

If Leo wanted to go upstream, Polly would head down and damn the consequences. Polly had a plan of her own. Her life was already on the line and the risk of rape seemed a small price to pay.

They had set off, she knew, in a flat calm. The faint breeze which they now had must therefore be the apparent wind caused by their motion over the ground as the ebb-tide swept them down-river. If she headed as close to the wind as she could, first on one tack and then the other, they would surely proceed seaward. The sail slatted suddenly. Behind Leo's back, a momentary puff of real breeze opened the mist and she glimpsed a high bluff and a row of caravans.

Polly made a cross on her mental chart and hid a smile. Her next landmark would be no more than a sound, the squawk of the seabirds which nested in their thousands on a rocky islet halfway to the sea.

THIRTEEN

Craythorne flicked a glance round the big shed. Everything seemed to be under control.

RSM Heather was firmly on guard, but all risk of opposition seemed to be at an end. Harry Moyes was preoccupied with his damaged throat. Clem Pilling had been fetched inside; as consciousness returned he was concerned with nothing but his broken wrist. Teeth was getting to his feet but shakily and with blood staining the lower part of his face. Ted Hancock, certain that he was hallucinating, had relapsed into sodden stupor.

Mark Filbustini crouched against the wall, rocking slowly, whimpering in agony and holding his ears to spare his ruptured eardrums. The major had not been gentle with him.

Craythorne darted out through the wicket. His quarry had vanished into the mist. There was no sound of footfalls, voices or a car, but the mist could have smothered such sounds. The moist, sandy ground, and the muddy sand below high-water mark, showed his own tracks and those of a godwit in search of lugworms.

Then he remembered the boat and saw that it had vanished. The tide could have carried it off. But, on the off-chance, he climbed the metal ladder which was bolted to the wall and which gave access to a short, roof-level flagstaff. The mist still hugged close to the water, and from this higher level he could see the tip of a mast drifting out and down towards the sea. While he watched, it waggled suddenly.

He jumped the last ten steps to platform level and stepped into the shed. Dr Westerly was releasing Peter Helinger from his bonds and Teeth had made it to his feet; otherwise nothing had changed.

'There was another gun,' Helinger said shakily. His head was still ringing from the concussion of the stun grenade. 'It went under that bench.'

'Well done.' The major retrieved the Walther. 'The big sod's away in the boat with the girl,' he said to Heather. 'I'm going to take the rubber dinghy.'

'Maybe you are,' Heather said. 'But take a look at it.'

The major looked. The dinghy was collapsing slowly against the wall. A fragment of bakelite from the stun grenade had passed through it. There would be time enough later for curses. It was too soon to invoke the civil authorities and thereby begin a process which would only end when the whole story had been picked over and publicised and society's concept of retribution imposed. The nearby locker was the obvious place for the repair kit . . .

The boy with the broken teeth was beside him. 'Can I help?' The voice was distorted by the damage to his mouth but the major understood him.

'I'll do this,' Craythorne said. 'You see if you can find a chart of this river while Dr Westerly goes back to the Land-rover. I want some smoke grenades and a compass.'

'All right,' Teeth said. 'But when this is fixed I'm coming with you.'

The major looked curiously at the boy and made up his mind. 'Bring a screwdriver,' was his only comment. 'And, Sar'nt-major . . .'

'Sir?'

'You might start thinking about how you're going to get this lot cleaned up.'

Heather looked around him and his jaw dropped. The second shot had hit a can of red antifouling paint, bursting it and sending a thin spatter throughout the shed. 'No problem, sir,' he said, wondering how on earth to begin.

Leo looked up. Somewhere above the mist the sun would be shining but he was damned if he could make out its direction. 'You sure you're on course?' he asked.

'Certain,' Polly said. 'I know this river like the back of my hand.'

For all his years at sea one piece of water, even seen close to, looked very like another to Leo. 'You better be right,' he said grimly.

'Buoy coming up. It should say Middlebank.'

Sure enough, a port-hand buoy loomed out of the mist. Leo read the name on it and was partly reassured. 'How long before we reach the first bridge?'

'Hours yet,' Polly said. 'The tide's still against us.'

'It'll turn soon,' Leo said. The water had been very low when they embarked. 'Are there any roads near the shore-line here?'

'No main roads. There might be a farm-road, for all I'd know.'

The feeling of being dependent on a woman was turning Leo's stomach. It was time to take her down a peg. 'You're all spots,' he said. In his experience, that was the most upsetting thing you could say to a woman.

'So are you,' she said calmly. 'I think it's paint. That's

going to make a problem for you, isn't it, if you want to get away without being remembered?'

'Shut up!' Leo said. He tried to scrub at the paint-spots on the back of his left hand, but the paint had dried on to the warmth of his skin.

'People are going to remember anyone as big as you and covered with red spots,' Polly said. 'That's the sort of thing people remember.'

Leo forgot his wound and jerked his left arm, stopping with a hiss at the pain. He took his knife out with his right hand.

'I told you to shut up,' he said. The screeching gulls sounded like his sisters' nagging whenever he had offended against the rules, while Polly sounded more and more like his mother, always reminding him of what would have been better forgotten. 'Bug me again and I'll slice you and put you over.'

'If you think you can sail this boat yourself and get your money back on your own, go ahead.'

It was always the same. If his head would only clear he could have found answers to her arguments. 'How do I know I can trust you?' he asked, scowling.

'That's up to you,' Polly said. She steered the boat in a curve until the boom gybed gently across. 'You can take the helm if you want.'

Leo looked at the featureless water and the enveloping mist. 'You carry on,' he said. He made his voice as threatening as he could, half-hearing the almost forgotten voices joined in a chorus of condemnation. 'But no tricks, mind. Remember what I told you.'

'I hadn't forgotten,' Polly said. 'Did you really leave your lady-friend to die?'

'It was that or snuff her,' Leo said. 'And I found I couldn't do it. Too tender-hearted, that's my trouble.' He tried to smile.

'It doesn't worry you?'

Leo waved away the very idea. 'I'll tell you what does worry me,' he said. He was only thinking aloud, trying to find a way through the difficulties which writhed like snakes in his mind. 'That shooter the wop turned up with. I took it off him once before. I recognised the hand-grips. Last time I saw it, I left it on the table in her room. If the Bill found her, they wouldn't've given him back an off-register pistol. So they found her. The brothers. I don't like that at all.' He stopped and listened. 'I hear another boat. Don't make a sound.' His knife was still in his hand, still open.

The breeze dropped away and they drifted in aimless circles. The buzz of an outboard could be heard, sometimes seeming closer, sometimes receding into inaudibility. When the breeze picked up again, Polly guessed that the tide had turned. She began to edge towards where the north shore should be.

Dr Westerly, conscious of a certain juvenile enjoyment in acting like the hero of one of the Westerns which had enlivened his boyhood, held Major Craythorne's revolver on the subdued group. Whether he would ever have brought himself to shoot any of them he rather doubted, but the question was unlikely to arise. Peter Helinger was on guard outside the side door with one of the captured pistols, while the sergeant-major had announced his readiness to sweep the surroundings with automatic fire at the first hint of trouble.

RSM Heather clung uncomfortably to the slope of the roof and peered over the ridge. At that level he was usually above the mist, which clung like wet tissue to the cold water under the calm, warm air above. Without the colour filters on the major's powerful, strictly non-issue binoculars, he would have seen nothing, but through the red filter the peak of the tall sail could sometimes be seen. It was showing now, like the tip of a shark's fin, and he took a quick bearing. The sail was invisible through his prismatic compass, but he thought that he was close. He pulled the chart out from under his chest. The sail vanished again.

He let the binoculars down on their strap and fumbled for the radio. 'Major, sir.'

The radio came alive, transmitting the interference from a powerful outboard. When the sound had died away, the major's voice came through. 'Yes, Heather?'

'There's a platoon of sappers standing by to come out with paint when we're ready. And I just got another sighting of the sail. If you've done six minutes at eight knots on oh-four-five magnetic, I think it's north-west of you now.'

The major's sigh came over clearly. 'It seems I've heard that song before. If I'm guessing my speed right and if the outboard isn't throwing this footling little compass off and if you're guessing the distances correctly, you could be right, give or take a hell of a lot. I'll try making smoke again. This time, I'll try throwing the smoke-flare as high as I can.'

'Roger.'

'Going up . . . now!'

Heather scanned the mist, switching between colour filters. There was a dark smudge on the face of the mist, almost in line with a distant hilltop.

'Got you, Major. And I saw the sail again. Trouble is, I can't see you both with the same filter, but I was near enough. Steer three-one-oh for . . . four minutes and then make smoke again.'

'Will do,' the major said. 'But I'm almost out of flares.'

* * *

153

A line of rocks came marching out of the mist, green with weed.

'I heard a car,' she said. 'Shall I take us in?'

Leo nodded. 'How you going to get that phone-number?' he asked suddenly.

'There are ways,' Polly said. The question had caught her unprepared. She thought frantically. 'Computers emit radio signals. We've only got to be outside a bank when they make a connection and tape the signals. I can decode them.'

Leo looked away but watched her out of the corner of his eye. The effort of thought was becoming almost too much for him but he knew that what she was suggesting might be possible for a well-organised firm of surveillance experts, but not for him. The last hope of his money reddened and died. Even if he could solve his immediate predicament, there would be no way to control an intelligent, female prisoner while she gathered and used the equipment. It was over. She would have to go and he would start again. At the thought, the voices in his head became shrill again.

Polly's mind had raced ahead of his. She watched him from under lowered lids and caught his sly glance. His secret thoughts might as well have been lettered on a cartoonist's balloon above his head. Only her wits could save her now. She had one card to play. She had no way of knowing Leo's history, but a woman knows when a man is scared by her femininity.

The boat nudged the rocks. Leo stepped ashore, crouching. Polly breathed again. He could have killed her while he was still aboard. She had been ready to jump for it, but whether she could have swum with her wrists shackled together was far from certain. She put the helm over, using the last of the boat's way. The current swung the bow out and the sail filled on the

154

offshore tack. Leo's foot slipped on the slime but he had a firm grip on the gunwale. He jerked his head. 'Come out of there,' he said.

'I'm all right here . . .' And then, with her crossed hands hooked into claws, she hissed and snarled and struck at his face.

For a second, Leo's nightmares had materialised. He jerked back, his shoulder flared, his grip slipped and the boat was out of reach. He looked sullenly across ten feet of water. 'I wasn't going to hurt you,' he said. 'Come back.'

'Like you weren't going to hurt your girl-friend?' Polly balanced the boat neatly with the mainsail just spilling the wind, holding almost level with him but drifting out. Her voice was shaking, but that no longer mattered. 'I think I should tell you that fishermen are always getting drowned off these rocks. You see, they don't reach the shore. The sandbank will be well covered by now even if you knew where it runs. And in slightly more than an hour there'll be six feet of water over those rocks. And a jolly good day to you.'

His shouts followed her but were soon muffled by the mist.

Polly thought that she might be lost. She had brought the boat round in what she thought was a semi-circle, intending to meet the shore again up-river from the rocks, but she was sailing on and on through the mist. Her sense of direction, which at first had been indomitable, had failed. She had no compass, no chart and no gauge of time so that she could only navigate by a memory of the chart and a vague assurance that, if the tide were now flooding, the apparent breeze must be down-river. But it would only need a swirl of current or a puff of real breeze to throw that primitive calculation out.

155

She knew those rocks and they were very near the sea. Had she missed the rivermouth? Was she sailing parallel to the coast? She turned and sailed close-hauled on the other tack. Of course, if she were outside the rivermouth the current would be different. When the haar set in, it stretched for miles along the coast. She was sure that she had sailed over this piece of water before.

'Major, sir.'

Wearily, Craythorne stopped the outboard. Radio communication was impossible while it was running. 'Yes, Sar'nt-major?'

'I can see the upperworks of a ship, coming up from seaward. Small coaster, it looks like. You must be close to the main channel.'

'I can hear his engines,' Craythorne said. 'I'll steer clear of him.'

'You can do better than that. The sail's changed direction again, on to a converging course. Follow the coaster up and I'll tell you when you're at the nearest point.'

Polly was near exhaustion. Her wrists were raw and she was shivering with cold. Her head swam with the endless staring at blank mist. She knew that she should take avoiding action, but the thump of the ship's engines came from all around. If it didn't run her down, should she follow it up? Or was it going seaward? She had no idea.

The high bows came out of the white and the side was sliding past. The bow-wave caught her head-on and the smaller boat reared up like a frightened horse and then slammed down with a creak of every timber. The jolt threw Polly down, stunned and winded. When she recovered her breath, she was too tired and dispirited to move. The boat was plunging in the ship's wake.

She roused herself when the dinghy bumped softly alongside and two anxious faces peered down at her. The major held a Sterling rifle. He laid it down when they saw that she was alone.

She moved her lips, but no sound came out.

'I'll look after her,' Teeth said. And he added, 'You can trust me.'

'I know it,' said the major. 'I'll take you in tow. Sheet the sail in hard and keep the tiller central.' He spoke into the radio. 'All's well, Sar'nt-major, and we're coming home.'

'Steer two-four-five magnetic,' said Heather's voice. 'And well done, sir.'

Teeth was unscrewing the clips around her wrists. His movements were tender, lover-like. 'Your poor face,' Polly said.

He smiled, showing the gaps. 'At least I'll be able to get smaller ones in now,' he said. 'They won't be able to call me Teeth any more. Curse of my life, those great choppers have been.'

She smiled back. 'I rather liked you with them,' she said.

Major Craythorne had finished attaching a tow-line. His face appeared again above the gunwale. 'Ready to go,' he said. 'But first, what happened to your enormous abductor?'

The disorientated feeling had gone. Her nausea subsided. 'He fell overboard and drowned,' she said firmly. 'I haven't the faintest idea where.' She kept on talking until the outboard re-started, just in case Leo's shouts should be carried on a quirk of breeze.

FOURTEEN

Until Billy Ember put a foot wrong, it looked as if Eddlestone, like most other policemen, would retire miserable, frustrated in the knowledge that his life's work had turned out to be no more than containment, with never a final victory.

Ember's arrest had brought Eddlestone fresh hope. The Filbustinis' various lieutenants had been in trouble before without ever incriminating their bosses, but Eddlestone paused and sniffed the wind and decided that this time he was going to be lucky or somebody's head would roll. Delegating all other business to subordinates, Eddlestone refreshed his memory from his file and then set off, using his rank mercilessly until he had Billy Ember all to himself – apart from a constable who was ostentatiously not listening – in a squalid interview room within uncomfortable sight of Wormwood Scrubs.

When Billy Ember saw who was waiting for him he felt his stomach sink. He was between the upper and nether millstones and no mistake.

'You've done it this time, Billy,' said Eddlestone.

'It's a fit-up,' Billy said with as much conviction as he could manage.

'Not this time. There's too much evidence. And the charges split up very nicely. Threatening behaviour. Assault and battery. Blackmail—'

'How do you make it blackmail?' Billy demanded indignantly. 'I never went in for the black. Never in my life. That's dirty.'

'Demanding money or money's-worth with menaces,' Eddlestone said. 'Vacant possession's worth money, isn't it? And, this time, the witnesses are going to talk. The brothers won't get near them without a squadron of tanks, even if they can find them, which I'd bet against. You're going up the river, Billy, for a long time.'

Billy Ember thought furiously and while he thought he sweated. He had a young wife. The brothers Filbustini were not generous towards the dependants of their incarcerated employees but they had been known to make other, less savoury, arrangements to ensure their support.

'That Joey Jones,' he said bitterly. 'You've got him coming up soon for that whisky hijack, and he'd say anything to get a better deal.'

'Exactly,' Eddlestone said. 'Think about it some more.' He shifted in his seat. His backside was getting too old for long sessions on hard chairs.

'I just wish I'd known it at the time. I'd've done him for keeps. I hate men like that,' Billy mused. 'Shop anybody to get themselves off the hook, they would. I suppose the court wouldn't buy him as an undesirable tenant deserving eviction?'

'With brass knuckles? Come off it, Billy.'

It was axiomatic that nobody grassed on the brothers, because their revenge was brutal, certain and usually final. But Joey Jones was in the squeezer. Billy Ember was also in the squeezer. On the other hand, it dawned on Billy that he was in a position to shop the brothers so totally that they need never be feared again. It was a whole new ball-game.

'I might have something for you, Mr Eddlestone,' he said tentatively, 'if you had something for me.'

'I thought you might,' Eddlestone said. 'So what do you want to say?'

'Say is one thing, tell's another,' Billy said. 'I've something to tell you. What I'd say when the time came ... I'd take your advice on that. But I want my missus a long way out of harm's way first and an easy deal for me on the other thing. And I want it from the DPP's office, not just your say-so. No offence, Mr Eddlestone.'

'That's understood, Billy my boy,' Eddlestone said. 'No offence taken. Not the least bit in the world. You'd like a cup of tea, wouldn't you?'

'I'm not bothered.'

'Yes you are.' Eddlestone caught the constable's eye. 'Here, son. Fetch us two cups of tea from the canteen.' He waited until they were alone. 'Now, Billy. Tell me what you've got to tell. And then, if you say what I want you to say, we'll see what we can do about this other little matter.'

A week later, Eddlestone was ready. It had been a busy week. Apart from his own endeavours and those of his team, he had spread his enquiries widely. He had an encyclopaedic knowledge of the other divisions and always knew who to approach so that the enquiry would reach the man on the beat or in the squad-car, the man who would know the answer.

Mark Filbustini could still hear certain loud noises, but ordinary conversation was beyond him. Major Craythorne's clap to his ears, delivered with trained hands and desperate force, following close after the explosion nearby of a stun grenade, had damaged his inner ears beyond repair. He would never hear, in the normal sense, again.

Because of this, and for another, more subtle, reason of his own, Superintendant Eddlestone decided to interview the two brothers together.

The Filbustinis came, grumbling but peaceful. Eddlestone was known to them by reputation and he was not a good man to cross. Their business might never get much help from the police – not since the last clean-up of corruption – but it could do without being singled out for harassment. They would never have come so willingly if the invitation had not suggested that it concerned only Billy Ember's arrest.

There was no solicitor present. The brothers were not inclined to spend their own money on lawyers. A trip inside for Billy, they had agreed, might suit them very well. Eviction artists were ten a penny, but the young Mrs Ember would make a very useful addition to their stable.

Eddlestone met them in an interview room which was just as grubby as the other but much better equipped. He was supported only by a sergeant taking notes, but others of the team were in touch with proceedings by loudspeaker and by a video camera. Their view was not good because the camera was hidden in the ceiling and looked vertically down. There was also a tape-recorder placed conspicuously on the table. Finally, Eddlestone had made sure that there was at least one comfortable chair in the room.

When they were seated, Eddlestone looked at Mark. 'I should tell you that this interview is being recorded.'

Mark looked at Pepe.

'I'll do the talking,' Pepe said. 'My brother's deaf.' He put a reporter's notebook on the table and laid a silver ballpoint beside it.

Eddlestone pretended to frown. 'That's too bad, but it comes to all of us in time. I have a problem myself.' He tapped the hearing-aid in his ear.

Pepe was not interested in the ailments of aging coppers. He leaned forward and pressed the stop button. 'Tapes can be edited,' he said.

'I'm sorry you feel like that,' Eddlestone said. Another recorder in the next room would still be turning. 'We don't edit audio-tapes.' Pepe's act would be damned well edited off the video-tape, though. 'If we don't tape, the sergeant has to work harder to keep the records straight.'

'That's tough,' Pepe said. 'What did you want of us?'

Eddlestone looked down at his notes. 'Are you the owners of Thirty-two Viewfield Terrace, Poplar?'

'No,' Pepe said. He scribbled a few words and showed them to Mark who nodded. The overhead camera scanned the words and reproduced them clearly on the monitor next door.

'It is about Billy,' said a small voice in the superintendent's ear.

Eddlestone could have recited the facts in his sleep but he pretended to look for another paper. 'That's funny,' he said. 'The rent-books give the owners as Longmarch Properties, with an address in a solicitor's office in Holborn.'

'What's that to do with us?'

'Longmarch is one of the companies owned by Hazlemere Holdings. Same address.'

'So?'

'The directors of Hazlemere Holdings are down as B. Bexley, J. Houston and Frederick Houston. Your sister Beatrice married Arnold Bexley the bookie. Josephine Houston is your cousin and she has a poodle known as Freddie.'

Pepe shrugged. 'So some relatives of ours have an interest in the company. Is that a crime?'

'Of course not. Does Billy Ember work for you?'

'Who?'

'Billy Ember,' Eddlestone said patiently. 'The man you were seen talking to in the Fox and Grapes, the Shoehorn Club, the Green Hill Social Club, the Warrender Hotel . . . Need I go on?'

'Oh, him,' Pepe said. 'We know him, that's all.' He scribbled a few more words in his notebook for Mark's benefit.

'We know Billy Ember. We don't employ him,' said the voice in Eddlestone's ear.

'Do you also own Seven, West Lane, Brent? Or, to put it another way, is that property owned by a company in which somebody – your sister's cousin's budgie, perhaps – somebody connected to you has an interest? Because we've traced a former tenant who swears that you both visited the place with Billy Ember when the question of redevelopment arose.'

Pepe shrugged. 'We were thinking of buying it. Billy came along for the ride.'

'So you deny that Mr Ember was employed by you as muscle for clearing properties you wanted cleared?'

'Most certainly.'

'How about your brother? Ask him the same question.'

Pepe wrote and showed it to Mark. The page was full. Pepe tore it out and put it in his pocket. There was a gleam far back in Eddlestone's eye. Those pages might be safe from him for the moment, but as soon as the brothers were under arrest he would get his hands on them. Whether a court would admit them as evidence was something else again but, supported by the video-tapes, it was worth a try.

'Tell him we didn't employ Billy,' whispered the little voice.

'We didn't employ Billy Ember,' Mark said. 'If he got up to any rough stuff, it was his own idea.'

'Do you own the butcher's shop known as Best Beef?'

Pepe hesitated, but for only a moment. The shop's manager was their own employee and he was straight. 'That one is ours,' he said.

'Ask your brother why he took Mr Ember with him when he went to look at defective insulation in the cold store last April.'

This time Pepe's writing took longer. He half-filled the page and tore it out.

'Best Beef. Cold store. April. Tell him you took Billy with you to advise,' said the small voice.

'Billy knows a lot about building,' Mark said carefully. 'We had trouble with the insulation. I took him along to get his advice.' He looked at Pepe for approval.

Eddlestone was finding it difficult to postpone his reaction to each answer until Mark gave it. 'Have you ever been in the flat above the shop?' he asked.

'Never.' Pepe's poker-face was good, but Eddlestone could sense a surge of adrenalin.

'You don't own it?'

'No. I can't be sure,' Pepe added quickly, 'that one of my distant relatives doesn't have shares in a company that owns part of it. I wouldn't know about that.' He fiddled with his pen.

'And your brother? Has he ever been there?'

Pepe seemed to be glad of the excuse to write again. This time he filled the page before showing it to Mark and then tearing it out.

'I think they found the woman,' said the little voice. (Eddlestone felt a warm glow spreading through his

164

chest.) 'Be careful. I said we don't own the flat. Tell him you've never been upstairs there.'

'I've never been to the flat upstairs,' Mark said obediently.

'An ex-employee of the shop says that she saw the three of you entering the lobby.'

'I don't remember,' Pepe said with great casualness. 'Perhaps we went into the lobby to look at the condition of the mutual wall.'

'With Mr Ember?'

'Of course,' Pepe said. 'He was our adviser about the insulation.'

'And not one of the three of you ever went upstairs?'

'Neither of us. I can't speak for Billy Ember.'

'Nor met Miss Venable?'

'No. Who's Miss Venable?' Pepe added quickly.

'The tenant of the flat upstairs. She seems to have died some weeks ago. She's just been found.'

Pepe was as taut as a fiddle-string, Eddlestone could tell. 'Poor lady,' Pepe said. 'But what has that to do with us?'

'Nothing, if you never met her,' Eddlestone said. 'Tell me, who were you referring to when you said "I'll kill the bitch"? In the Shoehorn Club it was, some time about July. Several of the members recall the occasion, because you sounded as if you meant it.'

'That was somebody quite different.' Pepe stopped dead. If he brought the girl into it, she would mention Leo Gunn. And Leo's unmistakable body might wash up at any time, if it hadn't done so already, with a bullet in it. A bullet from a Walther which was still back at the flat. Until that pistol joined the other on the bed of the Thames, the less said about Leo the better.

'I should warn you that this is a case of murder,' Eddlestone said. He waited. His words had been a signal. Two more men came into the room and stood waiting. 'I'll tell you how we see it,' he went on. 'You were in the process of selling the site to Hersham Holdings for a supermarket. You wanted vacant possession. Miss Venable refused to move. So you hung her on her living-room door and you went back once a day to ask whether she'd changed her mind. A steel plate was added to the door, to make sure nobody broke in and found her. But, very inconsiderately, she went and died on you. That's how we see it.' It was also how Billy Ember would tell the story.

'But there's no truth in it,' Pepe said. He tried to rise but one of the men pushed him down. 'And you bloody know it. Not that that'd bother you, you bastard! We're not saying any more, not without a solicitor.' Mark was watching him anxiously, not understanding.

'That's your privilege,' Eddlestone said. 'Unless you want to explain the fingerprints?'

'What prints?' Pepe asked sharply.

'The ones we found in the flat.'

'Impossible.'

'Inside the lid of a gold cigarette-case, for example?'

The girl's cigarette-case, Pepe realised suddenly, which Leo had walked off with. The mean bugger must have passed it on as a gift. 'A loose object,' he said. 'I could have handled it anywhere. Miles away.'

'The place seemed to have been wiped over,' Eddlestone said. 'But a steel plate had been screwed to the inside of the front door. We took it off. Your brother's prints were behind it. On the door as well as the plate.'

'As landlords—' Pepe chopped the sentence off.

'You've already denied being the landlords.'

'I was wrong. We've nothing more to say.'

'And the dead woman,' Eddlestone went on. 'It's amazing what they can bring up from dry flesh these

166

days. Iodine fumes and X-rays. Clever devils, these scientists. They found one of your prints on the lady's thigh. Was she another loose object?'

'Nothing to say.' Pepe was scribbling hard. He pushed his notebook under Mark's nose. Mark nodded.

'Looks bad,' said the little voice. 'Say nothing about the other matter.'

'What other matter?' Eddlestone asked before he could stop himself. 'No, never mind. And no more notes. We're going to separate you now, and after you've been cautioned and charged we'll see whether your stories agree with each other.'

This time, Pepe had to be helped out of his chair. His knees seemed to have failed him.

FIFTEEN

Dr Westerly, glad to be out of the danger area, spent the long vacation as the guest of a former graduate who now ruled over a group of islands in an obscure corner of an equally obscure archipelago. The discovery of minerals had tossed the economy into the melting-pot and skilled guidance was needed in moulding it into a new and more modern form.

When he returned, the new academic year was beginning. New students were wandering lost around the quadrangles. Faculty secretaries were badgering their deans for timetabling decisions which should have been made months before. The University's internal politicians were making and breaking alliances by the minute. It was a familiar and much-loved scene. And, to add to his contentment, nobody seemed to be looking at him as if he were in any way peculiar.

He found Polly Holt lunching alone in a corner of the Staff Club dining room. To his surprise, she had not backslid but was still dressed – or perhaps, he thought, disguised – as an attractive girl. She was looking out over gardens already baring themselves for winter, only late roses and the occasional flush of berries adding colour to the browns and faded greens. She jumped when he put his tray down in the unoccupied place at her table.

'You don't mind?' he asked politely. It would have taken more than wild horses to drag him away. He was desperate for news.

'Of course not,' she said and smiled. She seemed more poised and confident than he had ever seen her before. 'I'm glad to see you. There's something I want to discuss. How were things in the Lesser Faraways?'

'Rich and not sure what to do about it. More to the point, how are things here?'

'Much as usual.'

'No repercussions from our ... escapade? Nothing filtered through to the islands and I didn't want to draw attention by trying to get news. I had a ghastly fear that you were all under arrest and that they were suppressing the fact until I walked back into the net.'

'Nothing like that,' she said, laughing. 'Major Craythorne did quite a job of clearing up.'

'That much I knew,' Westerly said. 'He had me shuffling cars and people around all that night. No more visits from investigators? Or from crooks wanting the key of the vault?'

'Nothing. It's been very quiet.'

'I couldn't be more relieved.' Westerly ate in silence for a few minutes. He could not remember when food had last tasted so good. 'There is one other thing,' he said at last. 'Did you see this morning's paper? I read it on the train. It said that two men had been charged with the murder of a woman who was found dead in a flat in East London.'

'I saw it,' she said.

'From the few but unpleasant details given in the paper, it sounded familiar. Surely there couldn't be two such atrocities occurring more or less simultaneously?'

169

'God, I'd hope not!' she said.

'I gathered that you and that boy – Teeth, they called him, but with less than good reason . . .' Westerly broke off, nudged by something in her face and relieved for the moment to postpone a subject likely to prove contentious. 'Are you still in touch with him?' he asked.

Polly turned faintly pink. The addition to her household of a good-looking youth with small, straight teeth had been a nine days wonder among her colleagues. (Her mother, on the other hand, had been ecstatic that her ugly duckling of an only child had not only blossomed but had even embarked on a stable, although no doubt disappointingly platonic, affair with a young man who was prepared to read aloud by the hour.) 'Steven is studying hard,' Polly said defensively. 'We hope that he'll matriculate, the year after next.'

'Wonders will never cease,' Westerly murmured without being quite sure to which wonder he was referring. It crossed his mind that Polly was getting more than her money's-worth out of her new wardrobe and persona. Perhaps he could negotiate a rebate on his share of the expense. But there was a more urgent subject for discussion.

'During the slightly incoherent review which we held of the events of that extraordinary day,' he said, 'I gathered that you and Steven had heard the man-mountain confess to that crime.'

'That's quite true,' Polly said. 'He thought that she had had a hand in the disappearance of his money.'

'Quite so. And no doubt what you wanted to discuss were the ethics of the situation. You, my dear girl, with all the impetuousness of youth and the tender-heartedness of your sex, will be feeling the need to step forward and set the record straight. And all credit to you.'

170

Dr Westerly washed down the last of his chop with a mouthful from his quarter-bottle of wine. Polly tried to seize this chance to interrupt, but he waved her down. 'It will, of course, be against your instincts to stand by and to let these men be convicted of another's crime. It is, after all, only human instinct to intervene when it is in one's power to save another human being from disaster. But I do beg you to consider carefully.'

'I—' Polly began.

'No, let me finish. These men may be innocent of this particular crime, but there can be no doubt that they are bad men. In this day and age, I fear, a bad man of reasonable competence may expect, statistically, to be convicted of no more than one crime in ten. So these men, while they may be innocent of this crime, are undoubtedly deserving of the sentence.

'On the other hand, if you rush in where angels – such as myself – would fear to tread, justice will not be served. If some of the true story comes out, the rest will follow. Those two men will escape a punishment which they may not have earned but which they certainly merit, while we three will suffer for an action which was, at the end of the day, no more than diverting ill-gotten money to the best of causes. My advice, therefore, is to let sleeping dogs lie. Do not, on any account, go to the police.'

'I wasn't going to,' Polly said.

'You weren't?'

'Of course not. I'd have told you sooner if you'd let me get a word in. That wasn't what I wanted to talk to you about at all.'

'What was it, then?'

'I've been promised a Lecturership,' Polly said, 'as soon as a vacancy occurs. But in the present state of finances, that could take years.'

171

'You're not suggesting—?'

'Just once more,' Polly said. 'We've found a way to get the phone-number. Steven thought of it, actually.'

Westerly gave a yelp which turned heads as far away as the bar. 'You've got to be out of your tiny mind,' he said. He poured the last of the wine into his glass. 'Just as a matter of academic interest,' he said, 'how would you propose to go about it?'

172